Tomorrow's Another Day

Jessica—

Welcome To Columbus!

Deindra

D. Simmons-Corbett

Published by Another Day Publishing
P. O. Box 706
Reynoldsburg, OH 43068

ISBN: 978-0-9983030-0-0

First Printing November 2016
Printed in the United States of America

10 9 8 7 6 5 4 3 2 1

Library of Congress Control Number 2016919032

Dedication

Joylynn Ross, you are the surrogate mother of my project. After giving birth it required a period of incubation, of which you have never left my side. Your knowledge, skills, and guidance have been a true blessing to me. So much that I am going to continue publishing my thoughts and ideas in the form of future novels.

Acknowledgments

As I travel through life's journey, I think back on the people of whom my path has crossed. Whether it was a short period of time or if it has continued into this current day, each and every person has made some type of impact or impression in my life in one way or another.

Ms. Fields, my 6th grade teacher, educating us inner-city kids with compassion and grace.

Mr. Melvin Steals, my 10th grade English teacher, embraced our personal interests and taught not only English, but life lessons as well.

Ron "Monk" Gates Sr., my stepfather, raised us kids with unconditional love.

Grandma Ruby, our endless conversations and your words of wisdom always enlighten my spirit and ignite my soul.

Margo Simmons and Ron Gates Jr., growing up we may not have had much, but we had each other. As adults, our time spent is limited, but our love for each other is silently strong. I love you both!

Jackie Gill Washington, I will never forget all of the

long night talks and words of encouragement. We were partners. You have always exhibited endless love without judgement. A true friend until the end.

Deirdre Sewell Lofton, ever since that first day of nursing school, our lives have not missed a beat. We have ridden in the front seat of life's rollercoaster together, and still we stand!

Ericka Dowdley, you have opened your heart to me. Our families have united and become one. We both can admit that not everything in life is fair; however, we have each other to make it through. Your strength has driven me to strive for higher heights.

Connie Stewart, nursing ignited our union. Our conversations during report were always the highlight of shift change. We developed a sisterhood that will continue to strengthen for many years to come.

Deidre Palmer, you bring energy to dark places. Your kindness and sincerity are attributes to the beautiful person you are.

Corinee Jenya, our short-lived union has taught me the true meaning of working together and true love. You are so "beautifully you."

Priscilla "Prissy" Golphin, as single moms we did it, always remaining positive through the struggles. You extended your hand of friendship during a very dark time in my life; just an angel sent from heaven.

Shirley Gipson, you always made certain there was enough of "everything" for all. You wrapped your loving arms around your neighboring children and loved each and every one of us.

Sherri Igartua and Naashon Corbett, thank you for opening your hearts and welcoming me into your lives.

Shari Williams, Saundra Briscoe, Pam Mills-Simmons, Carla Moye, Debbie Moye, and Alisa Jeter Bender, our time together subsided throughout our life's journey; however, you all remain near and dear to my heart.

Marlene Brown, our journey began in the USAF and has continued today. United we stand!

Maxine Murry, I always looked forward to summer vacations with you and the family. Your expressions of love are electrifying and I cherish my childhood memories because of you.

Nicole McClairn and Sonya Franklin, thank you for all you do daily.

Jerry Ziglar, no one could ask for a better mentor, colleague, and friend. You have such a priceless way of showing me the ropes. I have certainly blossomed because of you.

Patrice Wilson-Walker, you followed the lead and now you are the leader. I am so very proud of you and your accomplishments. You are a perfect example of hard work and dedication paying off.

My daughters, Carmen Woods and Onrayia Wright, you both exhibit electrifying love to me. Just watching you grow up, develop your own personalities, and mature has kept me grounded. I have and will always be the best me because of you.

My husband, Ronald Corbett, your continuous support is so very much appreciated. You have allowed me to be me. You accepted all of my flaws and shortcomings while consistently holding my hand as I follow my dreams. You were the missing link in my life. With you as my husband, my journey has been declared blessed.

For my parents, Marcella Simmons Ward and William Robert Ward, because of both of you, there is a me. Your endless support and willingness to help has not gone unnoticed. Mom, I have learned unspoken lessons through experiences as well as your example of having little, yet giving all. I love you both with all of my heart.

Chapter 1

Something long and hard had kept me up all night. Now come morning, I must have hit the snooze button on my alarm clock at least three times, because it was five forty-five in the morning. I'd set the clock for five-thirty, which meant I should have been up fifteen minutes ago. With each tap of the snooze button I was granted five extra minutes of sleep. So yep, three times it was.

That third time must have been a charm, because now at least I was alert. It registered in my mind that I should probably turn off the alarm instead of requesting another five minutes. Who could blame me, though, if I didn't? It had been a long night, and I do mean *long*.

I'm sure everyone has experienced that kind of night and can relate to what I'm talking about. But at least this particular night didn't involve my usual something long and hard, if you know what I mean.

I'd been up until two o'clock in the morning; at least that's what time it was the last time I'd glanced at the clock before my eyes had finally closed for good. I'd been watching back to back reruns of my favorite TV shows from back in the day, *Good Times* and *Sanford and Son*. Prior to my mini TV show marathon, I'd gotten tucked away in bed and had actually fallen asleep at around 9:00 PM. But for some reason, I just could not stay asleep. Once I woke up, I could not fall back to sleep.

Knowing that each moment the clock ticked, it was getting closer to the time I had to get up to prepare for work. Yet that did not keep my eyes from staying glued to the television set. A long night of old reruns equaled me oversleeping. So the only long and hard thing that had kept me up all night was a damn remote control. Had it been a long and hard dick, maybe it would have been worth the exhaustion I was feeling.

I stretched my arms out. In one scoop I picked up both my cell phone and my pager from my Marni mirrored bedside table that I'd gotten for a steal at Pottery Barn. I found the specialty shop to be a little pricey. The only reason why I ended up in there in the first place was because I had to use the bathroom while out and about, and I didn't think I could make it home. Way in the back near the restroom was a clearance section. On that particular day it was an additional twenty percent off the clearance sticker. So I absolutely did walk out of that store with a piece of toilet paper stuck on the bottom of my shoe and a brand new bedroom suite for only a mere fraction of the original retail price.

Even though people thought that having MD behind my name meant that I had excessive zeros on my bank statement, I never confirmed or denied such with my lifestyle. I wasn't into labels or owning expensive things and furniture. I was very price conscious. I'd worked hard to earn the coins I did have, so I'd be dammed if I was going to toss them around like pennies in a wishing well.

I glanced at my hospital pager and saw that I'd missed two pages. I looked at my phone and saw that I had one missed call from the hospital.

"Ughhh!" Some days I wanted to say the hell with it all. Screw the job and screw having to get up at the crack of dawn to go to the job. But that would mean screw the nice little paycheck that came along with it as well. And screw the fact that I was living my life in the profession that some could only dream of.

It was true that I, Denise Simpson from the Valley Terrace projects of Aliquippa, Pennsylvania, was living my lifelong dream. Although I was a successful OB/GYN physician, I was definitely having a hard time separating my personal life from my professional one. Being a doctor meant true dedication and sacrifice. That had all come easy while I was studying to become a doctor. Back then I was laser focused, spending every night of my life studying. But that was then. Now I had desires of becoming a student of the nightlife. I'd missed so much with my head buried in books and cadavers.

After a long day's work dealing with my ratchet patients, the afterhours of nightlife is what mellowed me out. Unlike Olivia Pope who preferred to drink her fishbowl full of wine in the privacy of her own home, I loved the lure of the streets; the parties, drinks, and socialization. Once I started with a drink, several had to follow. This made it very difficult to get up every morning to fulfill my professional duties. Mix that with some old reruns, and it could become a deadly combination.

I loved my job, my patients—some of them anyway— and my colleagues, so every time I failed when it came to my professional life and goals, I was failing them. But I'd promised myself that I was going to get better this year. Of course that promise was made last week when I'd made my New Year's Resolution. Only a week in and I was still lacking in the punctuality department. The fact that it was well-known that there wouldn't be any consequences for my actions made the resolution—any promise to myself regarding my work for that matter—that much harder to keep. After all, I was Dr. Denise Simpson. The head chick in charge at Sentara Leigh hospital. I wasn't running the entire hospital, but I was running my modest office in the OB/GYN unit of the hospital.

I did not have to punch a clock. I was the boss of me as well as the couple of nurses and assistants under my authority. The days of me taking orders and being reprimanded were long over. I hadn't had to deal with that subordination issue since my earlier years as a commissioned officer of the United States Armed Forces. Heck, I'd paid my dues and now it was time to reap the benefits.

Most of my colleagues were born with silver spoons in their mouths, many of which were the offspring of plastic surgeons, Cardiologists, Endocrinologists, Neurologists, and the like. Their lives had already been planned for them at birth. You know that scripture about God knowing the plans He has for us while still in our mother's womb? Well, yeah, it was something like that, only their parents didn't care much about what God had to say about it. Their darling sons and daughters were going to work in the medical field or else. No other profession was an option. Forget about going to college and taking up dance or excelling in athletics to become a professional athlete or coach in a league. That would all have to end up being a hobby or a side gig.

It was very difficult for me to believe that most times some of my colleagues did not even attend lectures, yet they would get an A or B on exams. Not until I found out that their parents knew professors in high places did everything begin to make sense. My family was not composed of physicians, lawyers, engineers, or anything thought to be a profession prestigious enough to be amid the elite. There were no footsteps to follow in my particular field. I had to work my way up the ranks and basically do any and everything possible to succeed. And when I say any and everything, please understand that I mean that in the most literal way.

I was born and raised in Pennsylvania in a small city not

very far away from Pittsburgh. Most people have never even heard of the place. Aliquippa was a small city consisting of non-working or barely working low to middle class folks.

After J & L Steel Mill folded, Friday night football was the only thrill of the town. Everyone was excited about the high school football games. Every year coaches were grooming young athletes for the NFL. If one did not get out of the town academically, being a star on the football field or basketball court was the only other sure ticket out, and that pretty much only applied to the males.

Since I was the wrong gender for either sport, I decided to buckle down and study hard. Academics were my only option as far as I could see. My only way out was to get good grades, obtain a college scholarship, and fly somewhere far away from Pennsylvania. I wanted to fly; not walk, not run, not boat, not drive, or ride. You get what I'm saying? I wanted to go so far away that only a plane could get me there.

My older brother, Antonio, who was a little bit more academically challenged than me, decided he'd use football as his escape. He became the star running back at Aliquippa High School. As a starting freshman, which was unheard of at our school, he donned a jersey with the number twenty-one. He started every single game without fail. He obtained many school records with little effort. His name would go down in history for rushing yards and touchdowns. Antonio rushed over 1,000 yards in his freshmen season. He also scored fourteen touchdowns in that same year. What could I say? The boy had natural talent and I was proud to call him my big brother.

By Antonio's fourth and final year of high school, all the girls, faculty, and coaches loved and admired him. Even some of the guys wanted to be him. He was a C student, but with talent like that, his grades were oftentimes overlooked. Head coaches and scouts from the most prestigious colleges all around the United States were in contact with my mom in an attempt to get her to convince Antonio to become a part of their alma mater.

I'd like to say that out of everyone, my mother benefited the most from Antonio's athletic success; at least in his senior year anyway. Every time I walked in the door from school, I'd find something new. I came home one day and there was a new sixty inch television in our small, two-bedroom apartment that was shared by me, Antonio, my younger sister, and mother.

My sister and I shared a bedroom. My brother had his own room, as the housing authority prohibited children of the opposite sex from sharing the same room. My mom would make a bed out of the living room sofa. Most of her clothes and personal items were stored away in a shared closet in my brother's room. There was barely any room for us in the house, let alone this new movie screen that was now sitting in our front room.

The following week after the new television appeared, our refrigerator and deep freezer were filled from the bottom to the top. This was simply unheard of for our household. Even on the first of the month, nobody's stuff was stacked like that. Heck, where I came from, half the food stamps were sold before the head of household even went grocery shopping for their own home. Even without half the food benefits being hustled on the streets, food stamps allotted to a household of our size only provided meals for eighteen to twenty days out of the month. That was on top of plenty coupons being used.

The last two weeks of every month, our only meals were the free lunch provided at school and the free breakfast they offered if we weren't running late. But, uhh, as I mentioned, timeliness had never been a quality of mine, so by the time lunch rolled around, my hunger pangs were on ten.

We lived in public housing, which was a government subsided apartment complex, aka, "The projects." Most of the time utilities were included in our monthly rent payment. Since the monthly rental amount was based on my mom's income, any and everything was closely monitored by housing inspectors, apartment managers, as well as nosey neighbors and so-called friends.

Valley Terrace was not a community where neighbors would mind their own business. Everybody knew what was going on in everybody else's life. That place gave six degrees of separation a whole new meaning. Seemed like all the kids were cousins, brothers, sisters, or something. It was not uncommon for a local drug dealer to father two or three children by different females in the same apartment complex. There would be plenty of Ray-Ray Juniors running around. I personally could never understand why unwed women would name their children after a deadbeat dad. There was this one chick alone who had five children with four different last names.

My mother was a very private person, so she wasn't one to sit out on the stoop clucking her mouth with all the other hens. She certainly didn't talk about all of the gifts and contributions she received from the coaches and universities. She never had company or invited neighbors over, so no one suspected anything, that was until one day she picked my sister and me up from school in a brand new black on black BMW 325i.

"Dang, Ma," I said, approaching the car and running my hand across the hood. "Whose ride is this?" I was smiling from ear to ear. Just to be able to touch something this fancy had me tickled, never mind the fact that I was actually about to ride in it.

"Girl, whose you think it is?" my mother said with an air about herself. "And get your hands off of it. What makes you think I want your fingerprints on my car?" She rolled her eyes and looked straight ahead.

I'd heard the words she'd said, but I couldn't believe them. My mom could barely afford a monthly bus pass, let alone a brand spanking new car. And I knew it was brand new when I stuck my head inside and inhaled the new car scent.

"Mmm," I said with my eyes closed and a smile on my face. I didn't even want to open my eyes. Just in case all of this was a dream, I didn't want to wake up from it.

"Where'd you get it?" my sister asked, having taken the liberty of plopping herself in the front seat while I eventually climbed into the back.

"Yeah, where did you get it and how long do you get to keep it?" I asked, looking around the car and rubbing my hands down the butter soft leather.

"Well aren't you two nosey heifers just full of questions?" my mom asked, snapping her neck back while her eyes darted back and forth from my sister and me. "It's mine, it was a gift, and I'm keeping it until the wheels fall off." With that she threw that baby in drive and we floated off in style.

My sister looked over her shoulder at me with a knowing look. It didn't take a genius to figure out this gift, like many others, was compliments of one of the top three picks of schools Antonio had been interested in.

As we headed back to our apartment, I had one other question that I didn't bother asking my mom, which was, "How are you going to be able to keep the neighbors from noticing your new wheels?"

Meanwhile, Antonio was walking around feeling like a local celebrity, which he was in a sense. Grades or no grades, it appeared that Antonio was headed to whatever college or university he so desired. But if my mother had to choose, it would be the one with the highest bid. So upon receipt of her new car, that was that. The decision had been made. That same week my mom rolled up in that BMW, my brother signed a four year scholarship to play football at the University of Pittsburgh.

I was so thrilled, not only because our family received a bunch of nice gifts in the process, but he'd made it out. My brother had made it out of our small town and was headed to the big leagues. The day I watched him load the car the university had sent for him and ride off into the sunset, I made a vow to myself that I would be next.

It's not like our town was this godawful place where life there was torture. Growing up did not appear all that bad, especially when everyone around me was living in the same conditions as I was. It wasn't until my sophomore year of high school when I caught wind that we weren't simply low-income; we were poor.

I applied for a summer job at the Beaver County Training Center. The application required documentation of income. When my mother armed me with the needed information, I was speechless.

"What?" I remember saying to myself. Four people had been surviving off of $3,884 annually? I could not understand how this could be possible. I went as far as asking my mother how in the world she'd been pulling off what seemed like such an impossible feat. However, she did not reply. I concluded that perhaps she was embarrassed once I vocalized, in so many words, how poor our family actually was.

I guess the food stamps, free school meals, free medical insurance/Medicaid, zero car payment, and paying only $57 monthly for rent was about average in the projects. That was making out good. Heck, sounds like we had it made, right? Wrong! Because the minute I stepped out from the streets of the projects to the streets of the real world—downtown and Wall Street so to speak—oh I realized all too quickly that I'd been living well below poverty. Looking around at the white picket fences and the streets paved in gold—knowing I'd been living below par my entire life—brought out a fire and anger in me that made me want to go from the hood life to getting a taste of the good life; no matter what it took.

And so that's how I ended up where I am today, wearing the title of a doctor instead of a hood rat. I made it out, and with that fire still searing beneath me, I was going to continue to move forward in life, no matter who got burned along the way.

Chapter 2

After turning the alarm clock off this time and not simply hitting the snooze button, I lifted my body, which felt like deadweight, up off the bed. I grudgingly swooshed the covers off of me and swung my feet off the side of the bed. When my feet hit the floor, all I wanted to do was fall backward onto the bed and get five more minutes of rest. One more minute would have even sufficed. But that type of thinking, *just five more minutes*, was why I was in the predicament I was in now, which was late for work.

I may seem a little nonchalant about it, but I did hate being late for work. Even though I was always tardy and should have been used to it—right along with anyone else who knew my MO—I still hated the feeling it created inside. Being a woman of color only made it worse. Folks expected me to be late based on my African American descent alone. And there I was consistently proving them right. Ughhh!

I had a genuine ability and passion for my profession. It gave me such gratification when I delivered a baby without any complications. I honestly could not say that all my other colleagues mirrored my sentiments. I must admit, though, that late or not, I did my job well. I just had to get all the other hospital staff to understand and realize that my job was going to be done on my time. Not CP time (Colored People's time), but Dr. Denise J. Simpson's time.

It went without saying that all the years in the timely structured military made me defiant when it came to being punctual. In the military I was on Uncle Sam's time, well now . . . need I say more? And this was why I was in no hurry—as I peeled myself off the bed and dragged myself to the bathroom—to be punctual on this day or any other day for that matter.

In the military during my residency, it was not uncommon for the commander to assign a commissioned officer an additional twenty-four hour shift. When I say twenty-four hours, that is exactly what I mean. It was from sunup to sunup, not sunup to sundown. During those twenty-four hours, the only break I would receive was when the nurse was triaging a patient, and that was only if there happened to not be an influx of walk-ins, or during bad weather conditions.

I finally managed to get myself together and head to work. I looked at my watch as I pulled into the physician's parking lot of Sentara Leigh Hospital in Norfolk, Virginia. It was 7:45 AM. I was now officially forty-five minutes late. Not bad considering that when I was late, it was usually, at minimum, an hour late. Hmmm, I guess it would be a true statement to say that I was actually ahead of *my* schedule. My driving seventy miles per hour and pushing the pedal to the metal through those yellow lights had paid off.

Some physicians liked to go in a little early before their patients started arriving. They desired to have some wind down time in-between their commute and the plethora of patients and issues the day would bring. That wasn't the case with me. My shift began at seven, which was the exact time of my first scheduled appointment. Once I started off the day behind schedule, oftentimes it was impossible to catch up.

I always kept my fingers crossed for a cancellation or for one of my appointments to be running behind. The very few patients who had to report to their own jobs after their appointment with me were probably grateful for my failure to be punctual. That was more time they had out of the office. But those first-time stay-at-home moms who had a billion and one errands to run, now those were the ones who were sure to give me the side-eye.

There were so many people who would love to be in my position. Hell, I loved the position I was in. After all, this was my first "real" job after the OB/GYN residency program in the military.

I'd earned my undergraduate degree from The Ohio State University. I then continued my doctorate studies in the military. The military welcomed me with open arms when it became time to complete my residency, specializing in Obstetrics and Gynecology.

All of my hard work had now landed me as a staff physician at Sentara. I was an African American female with my own office in a hospital. How's that for a little Black girl from the Valley Terrance projects? There were other staff doctors as well. We were all assigned to different floors/clinics depending on our field of specialty.

My responsibilities included, but were not limited to, making rounds on the regular gynecology floors for routine pap exams, breast exams, and treatment of GYN diseases such as syphilis, gonorrhea, and venereal warts. I also rotated between scheduled and emergency C- Section deliveries, vaginal deliveries, as well as high-risk pregnancies, which included breech deliveries.

I was in the initial mental stages of working toward opening my own private practice. My position here at the hospital was the next best thing until I could settle down and start putting the things I'd only put down on paper into motion. More importantly, it was the perfect learning ground for running my own practice. I didn't have anyone breathing down my neck, and I was expected to run my clinic independently. Most of my planning was just that at this point; simply plans. And my plans were my dreams and ideas on paper that I hoped to manifest eventually.

Thinking about how lucky I was actually caused me to put some pep in my step. I briskly walked from the parking garage and into the hospital. By the time I arrived on the OB unit, the nurse on duty was right there ready to give me the rundown in order to catch me up to speed on things.

"Good morning, Dr. Simpson," the nurse greeted as soon as the door opened. She walked in unison with me as she read me the morning's medical report thus far. "Miss C is in delivery room number two ready to push. Mrs. P is in delivery room number three and is four centimeters dilated."

On the unit, we often referred to patients by the first initial of their last name instead of their full name. We were being compliant with HIPPA laws, a hospital wide federal regulation.

I kept a strong stride as I made a mental note of what the nurse was saying. Before I missed the delivery that was about to take place in room number two, I quickly scrubbed up and mentally prepared myself for the miracle of life; the birth of a baby.

After eight pushes and minimal coaching, we were blessed with the presence of a healthy, seven pound baby boy. Just like that, all of the ill feelings regarding my late arrival, if there were any to begin with, were dismissed and replaced with the joy of a new and innocent life.

I continued moving forward from delivery room to examination room until all patients had been visited. I delivered another baby, a girl, within the first three hours of my arrival. After that, the action slowed and I had time to catch up on emails and complete documenting my notes in the charts of the patients I had seen that morning. There had been no complications, thank God. Just smooth sailing.

I wouldn't dare try to take all the credit for how well things had been going. There was a great team of nurses and staff that worked on the unit. They would do everything under their scope of practice to provide patients with excellent service, especially when it came to buying time for physicians to show up.

Both nurses on duty today together had fifteen years of nursing experience between them under their belt. They each knew my bad habit of tardiness and probably worked from a list of prepared excuses to give to my patients as to why I was delayed getting to the scene. Some of the excuses on the list included me having a flat tire, lost keys, late getting out of a meeting or appointment with another patient, and a family emergency. I could always tell which excuse had been given to which patient based on the patient's greeting to me. For example, "Doctor, I'm glad you found your keys."

The excuses would be rotated like clockwork. However, the family emergency was not used as frequently. I did not want to speak a true family matter into existence.

The nurses knew that eventually I would be there. Late, yes. A no-show, never. There was only one time where I was *almost* a no-show. It was on the occasion when a first-time mom began unexpectedly crowning. Crowning is when a baby's head starts to emerge bit by bit during each contraction. Nurse Tasha Reese had to contact the on-call Obstetrician to let him know to prepare himself in case he had to deliver one of my patient's babies.

Tasha and the on-call Obstetrician had my private and home numbers and would not hesitate to use them when necessary. They'd used both numbers on that particular day

. . . to no avail. It makes me cringe every time I think about that incident.

Upon answering my house phone I immediately heard Tasha bark into my ear. "Bitch, wash your ass and get it to this damn hospital."

All I could do was follow her instructions. "Okay. I'm on it," I said in a raspy, low voice. There was dead silence on the other end. "Hello. Hello," I croaked. No one was there. I then hung the phone up and tried to catch my bearings. I'd been in a deep sleep, still half sleep when I'd answered the phone. On more occasions than one I'd jumped straight up out of a deep sleep, only to be dazed and ultimately give myself a headache. So I was mindful this time around of not having a repeat.

As fast as I could get my body to move, I sat up in the bed. I stared at my cell phone, and the house phone that sat right next to it, on my nightstand. I could see the number eight blinking on the caller ID screen of my home phone. That meant I had eight missed calls. I picked up my cell phone and noticed it had around the same number of missed calls. All of them were from Tasha's cell phone or the hospital. Tasha and the Obstetrician had been calling both my cell phone and my landline back to back. Finally, after realizing the ringing sound was not part of the dream I was having, I decided to answer the phone.

If the ringing hadn't woken me all the way up, Tasha's booming voice had certainly done so. I'd learned that when it came to work, there was no conversation between Tasha and me. She said what she had to say and that was it, totally unfiltered. I would never even respond, and it took two to have a conversation. It was useless to try to talk to Tasha when she was in turn-up mode.

Tasha had hung up in my ear, not willing to listen to any excuses I might have tried to give her. By that action alone,

I could tell she was beyond pissed, and for the life of me I couldn't figure out why. So what I was late. I was always late; at least two to three times a week. Why was she so upset about my tardiness this time?

After sitting up in bed I looked at the clock that read 7:10 AM. A sudden feeling of doom took over my body. Already ten minutes into my shift and still in bed, things weren't looking good. That explained why Tasha was so heated. Typically if she called me I could at least say that I was in the car and in route, but today, no such luck. It was evident in my voice when I answered the phone that she had awakened me from my slumber.

Seeing the time put fervor in me. I headed over to the closet and pulled my clothes from the hook on the door. At least I had the good sense to have everything I needed for my work day laid out to eliminate having to fish through my closet on top of already being late.

I quickly showered, put my scrubs on, and darted out of the door. I don't even recall arming the home security system or even closing the garage door. My mind was on autopilot. I focused on making it to the hospital in record time. There was no coasting five miles above the sixty-five mile per hour speed limit. Nope, that wasn't going to be enough this time.

I pushed eighty, risking the chance of being even later if pulled over by the cops, and getting an outrageous speeding ticket on top of that. Then of course there would be points on my driving record and the chance of my insurance going on up. But none of that played relevant in my mind. I feared that the punishment I was going to get from Tasha was going to be worse. No, Tasha wasn't my superior or anything, but she wasn't one to play regardless. And I loved her for that, because that's how true friends were supposed to be.

One of the nurses on my team had called Tasha to see if

she'd heard from me. That was a code in the hospital; we tried to help one another out whenever we could, so if it meant making phone calls or bailing one another out in any way possible, that's what we did. That had been Tasha's and my code long before Sentara.

Tasha and I grew up in the same hood. We were childhood friends who went to school together. We both played clarinets in the Fighting Quips High School band. She was actually the squad leader, which consisted of six chairs.

We were always at one another's house on any given day. I was a sophomore and she was a senior, so I looked up to Tasha. We were inseparable and had good old genuine fun.

Tasha was college bound, on her way to Duquesne University. She had her driver's license at the age of sixteen and her mom would give up the ride on a daily basis. She even had the fortune of having a loving grandmother in her life.

At granny's house is where we did most of our dirt. Granny could not hear or see well, and on top of that, she went to bed by seven PM, which was perfect timing for Tasha and me to start finding something to get into. And believe me when I say we always found something to get into. Due to the fact that Granny was a heavy sleeper, we had parties right in her basement without her ever knowing about them. But then again there was that one . . .

I can remember one party in particular we threw one night after football practice. Tasha and the love of her life, Clarence, were on one side of the basement singing to the likes of Boys to Men and Whitney Houston, while drinking whatever cheap liquor our money pieced together could afford. I was in another room of the basement bumping and grinding with my guy.

My very last bump was when I heard a loud thump-like smacking sound. Upon hearing the sound I was startled, and from the loud yelp my dude cried out, it sounded as if he was in pain. Confirmation was the distorted look on his face.

I looked up to see Granny holding one of those black, wrought iron frying skillets in her hand. My date tried to rub his back of which the pan had obviously connected with.

Damnnnnnn, is all I could remember thinking. Over the slow jams that were playing, not one of us had heard Granny creep into the basement. But we all heard her public announcement.

"If you are under eighteen and not paying any bills in this house, I would advise you to get your shit on and get the hell out of here before I make it upstairs to pick up my phone to call some parents."

The four of us were scattering like roaches when a light gets turned on. We all made it upstairs and out of the door in record time. However, I still can remember the conversation Granny was having with herself as we exited.

"Those fast-ass girls are going to turn out just like their good for nothing mothers. Knocked up before they even out of high school! These boys don't want nothing but their cookies and milk. One day they will understand not to give that milk away free, especially when the cookie begins to crumble."

Even though Granny was roaring like a lion, I could sense the compassion underneath it all. Granny did not want Tasha and I to become teenage mothers like both my mom and Tasha's mom had been. My mom was a senior in high school when I came along. Tasha's mom had barely graduated high school prior to giving birth to Tasha, but she was still only seventeen years old.

Tasha and I heard Granny loud and clear, but we weren't listening at the time. Like any other normal teenage girls, all Tasha and I cared about was having fun. Man, oh, man did we have some good times. Well, maybe not all good, but memorable none the less.

It was a sad day when Tasha went off to college. I honestly thought I'd never see her again, but our memories together I'd have forever. At first we stayed in touch through phone calls and birthday cards, but eventually they became few and far in-between. So when I ran into her after ten long years of no communication, it was tripped out. I was in the cafeteria of Sentara and I heard that soft, electrifying voice.

"And I'll take a large drink too," she'd said to the cashier. And it was those very words that drew my attention.

Tasha had always had this southern accent like she'd been raised in the south. I would know it anywhere.

I paused for a moment thinking, *Couldn't be.* Then I looked up from my food and low and behold it was my girl Tasha right there in the flesh.

"Tasha! Girl, what are you doing here?" I said as I got up from the table and raced over and gave her a hug. My first assumption was that she was in the hospital visiting someone. I didn't even notice the scrubs she was wearing underneath her long, buttoned up sweater. It was always chilly in the hospital cafeteria no matter the season outside.

After using our thirty minute lunchbreak to talk for an hour, I was enlightened on almost all that had transpired in Tasha's life over the years. Neither of us could have cared less about any repercussions that might have existed as a result of our self-extended lunchbreak.

"I'm the nursing supervisor here on the OB/GYN unit," Tasha informed me.

I was excited to learn that she had begun employment at the hospital three years prior as a regular floor nurse, and rose above the ranks in one year's time. That accomplishment in itself was something to be celebrated. That's something that

Tasha and I had always done as sister-girlfriends, and that was to celebrate one another's accomplishments.

After hearing her good news, I paused for a moment. "Wait a minute. You work in the OB/GYN unit too? I'm not going to believe that we've never crossed paths in the hospital." I had been assigned to the sister hospital the first six months of my employment and had only been transferred to Leigh less than a month prior. But still, there was no way I could have seen or heard Tasha and not have known immediately who she was.

"I've been on vacation," Tasha said, which explained everything.

We hugged, laughed, and reminisced about Quip. The main topic of our discussion was when she shared with me that her high school sweetheart of ten years, Clarence, had traded her in for a different type of sweetheart. It came in the form of a white, solid rock.

The two of them had been together since her sophomore year in high school.

"We made our relationship work even while I was dealing with the load and pressure of college," Tasha had told me. "But after graduation, and once we moved in together, things started going downhill."

Tasha was still quite emotional while filling me in on her life's schedule of events. I was floored by all that she'd been through. It was like a part of her had died over the years. She wasn't the free spirit I had remembered her being. It was time for my dear friend to live again. And there was one thing I could say about myself; no matter what I was going through in life, I was gonna live.

Let me just say, though, that up until recently I hadn't felt as though I'd really been living life. Even now some may not consider what I'm doing as living; some may even consider it outright reckless. I wouldn't snatch up Tasha by the collar and drag her. I'd take baby steps with her. I could tell that it wasn't going to be an easy task bringing Tasha back from the dead. But if Jesus could pull it off with Lazarus, heck, anything was possible.

Tasha never had any children nor had she dated much after the breakup between her and Clarence.

"Since the breakup, I've buried myself in work to hide the pain," Tasha had shared.

I could tell by the tears forming in her eyes that our talking had clearly made all her past relationship hurts resurface.

"So how's the family?" I asked cheerfully, trying to switch the subject. I didn't want a black cloud to form over our happy reunion.

Tasha shared with me that her family still remained in Aliquippa. My mother still resided there as well.

"Most of my time and energy is devoted to my job." Tasha shrugged as if there wasn't anything better to do than work her life away.

That would explain the reason why she became the head of the department in just one year. I wish I'd been there for Tasha when life was happening to her, but I was here now, and that's all that mattered.

We exchanged phone numbers that day in the cafeteria and had been hanging tight ever since. We were reunited, just like the good old days. Yet, we understood our boundaries at work on a professional level. But in evenings and on the weekends, it was on!

There were many secrets shared between us, including secrets of how our after football practice parties had led us both to the abortion clinic. It's funny, because Tasha's mom would always remind us how our lives mirrored one another. She would have died had she known just how much they actually had.

The secrets Tasha and I shared didn't stop there. Nope, they continued on with us even trying pot for the first time together. But those secrets and memories were all in our past as youths. Needless to say, there would be plenty more secrets to keep as adults. The thing was, would they be secrets we shared with each other or kept from one another?

Chapter 3

Although my day had started off rushed and bumpy with me being late to work and all, everything was starting to smooth out. All of my medical notes from the morning deliveries had been completed, and my emails were answered. I'd been working non-stop since arriving at the hospital, which meant I hadn't even taken a break to eat, and trust and believe my stomach was reminding me at least every five minutes that it was running on empty. It wasn't the stomach pangs that were becoming so annoying as much as the loud, growling noise my stomach was making.

Upon logging out of my emails, I made a quick trip to the cafeteria where I grabbed me a nice Cobb salad to tide me over until after work, when I could really smash some food. Living alone, I preferred to eat out. I found it quite difficult to cook for only one person. I wasted more of the food than I consumed. I had this thing about leftovers; if I didn't eat them the next day, they were getting scrapped. I considered the food old at that point. Alone or booed up with kids and a dog, who in the hell wants to eat old food?

Yeah, eating out can be expensive, but I'm not talking about feeding a family of four. It's just me, and considering it was like throwing away money anyhow when I pitched leftover food, might as well throw it away on fast food. At least that I was going to eat.

After my quick lunchbreak, once I arrived back to my office I was greeted by a waiting room full of patients there for their scheduled appointments. Two of my patients who were ready to deliver had been admitted to the hospital as well. There was a first-time mom who was young, single, and scared to death. On top of all that, she was alone. I swear the maternity unit was starting to look like the visiting room of a women's' prison. Hell, you go to a men's prison and every wife, fiancée, mama, and side-chick is up in that piece. Where were all the ride or die fellas at when it came to the women?

At least the scenario was different with my other patient. She was a scheduled C-Section. This would be the third child born to the loving couple. The father was actually a surgical technician in the operating room. It was an honor for him to allow me the privilege to assist in bringing his child into the world. And it was definitely a step up from my normal cast of patients.

The first-time mom was nine centimeters dilated after having been in labor for only two hours. That was almost a record as far as any of my patients were concerned. A colleague said that a patient of his arrived at the hospital and was delivering her baby after only being in labor for an hour. But he suspected she'd been in labor at home for quite some time. She'd claimed that she'd immediately headed to the hospital after her water had broken. A nurse heard her telling one of her visitors the long laundry list of things she'd done prior to deciding to come to the hospital.

I knew for certain that wasn't my patient's story. Every time she got a cramp—anywhere on her body—she was running up to the hospital in false labor. Throughout her months of prenatal care, a long, miserable, painful labor had been her fear. She'd prayed to God that would not be her situation. I guess God answered her prayers and kept her from having to endure such an experience, because only two hours after arriving at the hospital and being in labor for real this time, she was ready to push. Not even ten minutes after her first push, I'd guided her to the delivery of her seven pound, ten ounce baby boy.

The scheduled C-Section began shortly thereafter. Just as with the first patient, within two hours this couple also became proud parents. The mother gave birth to a six pound and eight ounce baby girl. It was a good day in my unit if I had to say so myself. Not a single complication; no excessive blood loss, no additional orders to write. It was smiles and laughter, and the joyful cries of a baby's first means of communication outside the womb. I had to brush my shoulders off because I was truly feeling myself. My oversleeping and rushing around had not set the tone for the day.

After both delivery rooms were full of "thank yous" and tears of joy, I congratulated each family and excused myself as the mothers were then transported to their recovery rooms. I was headed to the High Risk Unit to check on the females who had been admitted, but then, low and behold, my pager went off. I sighed as I read the words on the pager: "GYN exam ready in room 1."

Change of plans.

I sighed as I changed directions, now heading to examination room one to check on that patient. "Can a sistah get a break?" I mumbled under my breath. "Am I the only doc responding to pages?"

There was one other OB/GYN on staff with me today. Why couldn't he have gotten the page instead of me? Or she? Hell, my day had been so busy that I had no idea who the other doctor on staff was. Right now I was too pissed to check. My only hope was that just like every other patient I'd seen today, this one would be smooth sailing as well.

I returned the page to the unit secretary, informing her that I was in route.

"Please don't let this be someone ready to deliver," I prayed out loud.

If I were lucky, examination room one would be a false alarm. I could stick a finger or two in the patient and send her home packing. Those false alarms were the worst, because usually the patients had phoned me prior to arriving at the hospital. I'd given them instructions to stay home, yet they'd high-tailed it to the hospital anyway. These unanticipated examinations would sometimes put a monkey wrench into my entire day's schedule. Those patients who had expected to come in and leave with a baby ended up doing nothing but wasting my time and theirs.

It was usually the first-time moms who pulled this little stunt. Repeat moms were in no hurry to get to the hospital. They knew better; they knew that if there was a chance that they were going into labor, they needed to finish laundry, because it was sure to pile up for the next three days while they were recovering. Nine times out of ten their significant other and children were going to leave it all for her to do. Might as well knock out all she could beforehand. And the repeat moms knew to grab one last meal before heading to the hospital as well. Because once they stepped foot in the hospital, it was nothing but ice chips until they gave birth, which could typically be hours from the time they walked into the door.

But no; the new moms just couldn't take heed to my advice over the phone and keep their asses at home. Some of them would have the nerve to get a little beside themselves when I'd confirm to them that it was a false alarm. That's until I'd send them home childless other than the one still in their womb.

During my residency, I hadn't been this bitter when it came to first-time moms and their repeat visits to the hospital with false alarms. More than likely it was because those folks were of a different working class than the patients I was now dealing with. They were lower-middle class, working people. Many of them were professionals and corporate folks who worked until the very end of their pregnancies. They were trying to hurry up and dump their loads so that they could get back to their regular work routines, some involving travel. And of course pregnant women were advised by their doctors not to travel after their sixth month of pregnancy. These women were not sitting around all day waiting for a check from Uncle Sam to arrive in the mail . . . not like the ones I mainly dealt with.

My roster of patients seemed to be filled with welfare recipients, Obama Care recipients, and folks too lazy to sign up for either and came in their ninth month of pregnancy wanting to set up payment plans. I might get the first three months of the one hundred dollar payments I agreed to accept, but then after that every dime the poor mother had, and I do mean poor in every sense of the word, went on diapers. It went on Similac as well if she was too lazy to sign up for WIC (Women, Infants, and Children). WIC is a program for women with children of a certain age that provides grocery store vouchers that allows them to purchase their basic nutritional needs.

The hospital and their staff had it worse than me. They'd get stuck with a $50,000 hospital bill that they ultimately would have to charge off. Taxpayers ended up eating that cost. I suppose that's what people meant by being your brother's keeper. I work too damn hard! I only want to take care of me and mine. Isn't there something in the Bible about if you don't work, you don't eat? Well, hell, that should go for having babies too. If you don't work, you don't have babies.

"Lord, I repent in the name of Jesus," I said, drawing an invisible cross over my chest with my index finger. How could I have such cruel and selfish thoughts? I have come to believe that the bitterness was beginning to take over me. In being honest with myself, I'd have to admit that it's not just my patients that have me feeling some kind of way, but it's my own life.

Working in Norfolk was a constant reminder of the poverty-stricken childhood I had escaped from. When most of my patients pulled out their state's Medicaid card for care, I'd cringe. Very seldom did anyone have a Blue Cross/Blue Shield health insurance card. It was only a small number of patients who even had Obama Care for that matter. I was beginning to feel as if I'd escaped the ghetto and now had returned to provide patient care there. In deciding to look at the glass as half full instead of half empty, at least I was on the giving side of things rather than the receiving end.

It's not that I discriminate when it comes to one's financial status; I think it's the attitude that comes along with some of my patients that gets to me. It baffles me how so many of them have this selfish attitude and sense of entitlement. Sometimes the attitude alone makes me want to pop off.

I had this one expectant mother who showed up right when my shift had ended wanting me to check to see if she'd dilated any.

"Did your water break?" I had asked her.

"No," she replied, shaking her head.

"Are you having contractions?"

She gave me the same reply as before.

"Bleeding?" I was grasping for straws now. I mean, what had to be going on that she decided to come up to the hospital without any signs, symptoms, or complications?

"Nuh, huh." She shook her head.

Okay, it was time for the million dollar question. "Then, honey, why do you want me to check to see if you have dilated?"

"Well, my boyfriend and I had sex earlier and he said it felt different." She leaned in and whispered. "Like my stuff wasn't as tight as it usually is." She then pulled back and gave me a knowing look.

What the hell did she think I knew? "*And*," I said, waiting for her to get to the point.

"And I figured I must be dilating, so I wanted to come in and have you confirm if I am or not."

"Bitch, bye," is what I wanted to say, but I had to remember which hat I was wearing, and it was that of a doctor. Now had I been on that *Married to Medicine* reality show, that response might have been acceptable, but since this was the real world, I thought better of it. "Honey, your insurance is not going to pay for an examination based on your boyfriend's estimation of the tightness of your vagina walls. So unless you want to pay for it out of pocket-"

"You mean to tell me Medicaid ain't gon' cover it?" She threw a hand on her hip, snapped her neck, rolled her eyes, and sucked her teeth. She then flung her blond hair over her shoulder. "This insurance is so whack it don't make no sense."

I had to bite my tongue. She was standing there as if she was actually paying a monthly insurance premium, a deductible, and copayment for her visits. I swallowed the words I really wanted to say, damn near choking on them. I painted on a smile and then repeated myself. "I can do the exam, but you will have to pay for it out of your own pock-" I couldn't even get the full word out this time.

"Oh, no." She was quick to cut me off. "It's all good."

She went just as quickly as she had come.

I didn't care if she had answered yes to all the questions I had asked her, me examining her was not going to go down. The little hand on the clock happened to be on the five and the big hand was a few strokes from hitting the twelve. I may get a late start on my day every now and then, but if I could help it, my day always ended right on time. I just had to let these patients know what time it was, literally and figuratively. But not every case was as simple as that.

Some of the patients I'd been dealt in my hand by life were ghetto and ratchet to the tenth power. They were a product of their living environment, which was my work environment.

The hospital was centrally located in downtown Norfolk. I would venture to say the bulk of patients seen here were below poverty to lower class. Most were on public assistance or working dead-end minimum wage jobs just to make ends meet. It was a rare treat to notice a patient presenting a Blue Cross Blue Shield card instead of the local county Medicaid card. That meant I was going to get paid my worth. And please don't get me wrong; allow me to reiterate that I have nothing against folks who can barely keep their heads above water. That could have easily been me, and that's probably why I feel the way I do. It's not necessarily hate I'm feeling. It's the remnants of my childhood fear; the fear of living in the projects getting by with making $3,884 annually.

I despised just the thought of living the life my mother had lived when I was growing up. I still do. So it's not the patients I can't deal with, it's that little girl inside of me that I can't deal with. That I don't want to deal with.

One thing I do know is that even if I hadn't ended up on the right side of the tracks, my broke ass would have at least been humble and grateful. Some of these people I encounter have no couth whatsoever. Once I finally meet the trees the apples have fallen from, I know exactly why they are the way they are.

I had a patient that was only fourteen years old; child had a mouth like a sailor. When she first started coming to see me, she let the white coat and the white voice I use when it's about those coins fool her. Little girl even went as far as trying to threaten me. She pulled the "boss card" on me one visit, requesting to speak with my supervisor because she did not appreciate my tone.

"Sweetie, I am the boss," I told her with a painted on fake smile.

"Yeah, right!" she spat, puckering her lips out. "Yous a black woman, and what I do know is that ain't no goddamn body gon' let no darky be the boss of a whole damn hospital. Black folk ain't got no money to be owning no fucking hospital."

I was so used to her little ass by now that my mouth didn't even fall open in shock at the words she was spewing. "I know pregnancy can make you a little cranky," I said to her, still trying my best to be pleasantly professional, "or perhaps you simply woke up on the wrong side of the bed this morning, but I'm going to need you to-"

"Me woke up on the wrong side of the bed?" she poked herself in the chest so hard with her coffin shaped acrylic nail, I thought she was going to puncture a main artery.

That would not have been a good thing for her. She and I were the only ones in the examination room at the time and I'm almost certain that I would have let that little bitch lay there and bleed to death.

"Speaking of beds," she continued, now pointing her finger at me. "You have a terrible bedside manner."

Oh, so now that heifer wanted to use a phrase I could comprehend, minus all the double negatives. I wanted to ask her to spell *bedside manner.*

I took a couple breaths because I realized that she was pregnant and probably a little edgy. But somebody needed to tell these folks that once the clock strikes five, oh, the scrubs hit the floor and I'll get in that ass. But to date, no one had taken me quite to that level . . . not yet.

I tried my hardest not to let that child or anybody else take me there and jeopardize my career. My tardiness could be overlooked, but catching a case for clocking one of these hoes upside the head, not so much. Besides, the poor girl didn't know any better. Like I said before, I'd met the tree.

Her mother had walked in the room during a vaginal examination very proud and eager to see her grandchild born into the world. "My baby is having a baby," the mother had said proudly, smiling from ear to ear. "I'm 'bout to be a granny! I'm gon' be the finest granny dese folks eva seen in these parts."

I thought to myself, *What a damn shame.* This child should be in school learning geometry or some shit like that. Instead, her rusty butt is up in stirrups and her own mother doesn't see the problem with that. I could not understand how these thirty-something grandmas would step up in the hospital and brag about how cute their grandchild was going to be and how the drug dealing baby daddy bought this, that, and all of the other. These teenage girls should have been getting something in their heads instead of between their legs. In my mind, I'm sorry, but I did not see it as a blessing from God. I saw it as another one of my tax dollars in the contribution bank supporting unwed mothers' children. But thank God I loved babies. Can't blame them for their ignorant ass trees . . . I mean mamas.

In dealing with the fourteen year old turn-up queen, I remained the bigger, older, more mature person and examined this baby who was about to have a baby. She had dilated two centimeters. I instructed her to return to the hospital if and only if her water broke, she began having contractions, or if she noticed any signs of blood. Both the youngster and her mother verbalized their understanding; however, that meant nothing. I expected to see them both pop up in the hospital within the week as if they had a schedule appointment.

In thinking back to that incident, I said a silent prayer that the patient awaiting my arrival on the High Risk Unit would be nothing like my norm. I don't know if I could deal with the drama right now.

The main hallway of the hospital was where everyone entered the elevator going to the even numbered floors. The eighth floor was my destination. I pushed the 'up' button, and fortunately I didn't have much of a wait. Within seconds the elevator doors opened. I went to step in but then damn near stopped in my tracks. I couldn't move. I couldn't blink. I could barely think. *What was I supposed to be doing again?* I had to ask myself.

"Going up?" the voice broke my trance. His voice; the one that belonged to the occupant already on the elevator.

I swallowed the lump in my throat and managed to say, with a head nod, "Uhh . . . umm . . . hmm, yes." But still I couldn't move.

He waited a few seconds and then said, "Then do you want to get on?"

I looked around, realizing that I had my right foot in the elevator and my left foot still out of it. "Oh, yes. Sure, sorry." I let off a nervous chuckle and then quickly allowed my left foot to join my right one inside the elevator.

"Which floor?" he asked as I entered.

His voice sounded as smooth as his caramel skin complexion skin. It was a perfect mixture: not too light and not too dark.

"Eight please," I answered.

Before I did my 180 to turn and face the closing elevator doors, I got a quick look at the name printed on his white lab coat. *Dr. Cannon.*

Was this fine specimen of a human being real or a mirage? I mean, it had been a week since I'd been intimate with the opposite sex. For me that was too long. So maybe I was seeing things; imagining myself secluded in an elevator with a man who didn't even have to buy me Red Lobster before I'd give him some cookie.

Where had this Dr. Cannon come from? I mean, clearly since he was going up he must have ridden the elevator from the basement, which we also called the lower level. But that's not what I meant by where he'd come from. I had never seen him in the hospital prior to this moment. Trust me; I would have never forgotten his handsome face. Was today his first day? Why hadn't we run into each other before now? Was he a resident or on staff? My mind was forming one question after the other. My thoughts were moving just as fast as the elevator was climbing floors.

Ordinarily I was anything but speechless. I wouldn't have hesitated to ask any other doctor the questions that were circling my head. But ole Dr. Cannon here wasn't any ole doctor. He was so damn fine that he'd rendered me dumbstruck. I couldn't even say the alphabet, let alone put together letters to form words. Complete sentences were out of the question.

Through my peripheral vision I could tell Dr. Cannon was looking straight ahead, watching the numbers light up on the screen above the elevator doors that displayed each floor we arrived at and passed. As he waited for the doors to open and deposit him onto his floor, I turned my head more toward his way, as if I was looking at the number panel beside the elevator doors. In all actuality, I was scoping him out as best I could.

I noticed that he was very well groomed. Nothing was out of place. His teeth were as white as pearls. I'd noticed that when he'd spoken to me. He smelled delightful. The aroma was that of a fresh, powerful magnitude of deliciousness; so soft and divine. He was carrying two lab coats that were in plastic and thrown across his left arm, clearly a result of a dry cleaners run.

Under his lab coat he was wearing a navy John Varvatos suit. I recalled that this particular designer had stores in Las Vegas, Los Angeles, and San Francisco; all other business transactions were conducted online. He also wore a light gray shirt. The tie perfectly matched his suit. His total ensemble made my mind wonder beyond the waist. I allowed my eyes to lower without moving my head. From what I could tell, his shoe size looked to be about an eleven. And we all know what they say about a man's shoe size. I shivered at the thought of his snake on the plane landing on my runway strip.

I could not help but notice the fashionable cufflinks that were engraved with the letters "RC."

RC, I said to myself. His last name was Cannon, so the R must have stood for his first name. It could have been Robert. No, he looked more like a Rico, or maybe Richard, or even Rashaun. I wasn't sure, but I was definitely not going to be able to rest until I found out this man's full name. Who better to ask than Tasha?

I was still considered a new kid on the block at the hospital. Tasha had been working at the hospital way longer than me. She knew all and would tell all simply by me asking. Around these parts, no one had to dial 411 for information. Tasha on speed dial sufficed. I made a mental note to text her the first moment I had free.

If I had not known that this man occupying the same space as me was a physician, I would have sworn that he made a living as a professional model. He reminded me of a model for *GQ* magazine with fifteen years maturity over the normal models-for-hire that would appear in the magazine.

In having looked at the door panel and noticing that the number eight was the only floor lit up, I wondered if that meant he was headed to where I was going. Perhaps he was an OB/GYN. Any woman would love to spread eagle for their annual exam for that man. It would be easy to let his size eleven man part glide into my inner self. The KY jelly lubrication would not be necessary. His mere appearance would make any female moist between the legs. Once again, I quivered inside. Whew! This man was going to make me have to change my panties.

That fifteen second elevator ride felt like a vacation. When the light lit up and announced that the elevator had arrived at the eighth floor, I didn't want to exit into reality. I wanted to extend my vacation in the form of an elevator ride with Mr. Fantasy. Knowing that wasn't possible, I stepped off of the elevator, waiting to feel his presence behind me.

"Oh, shoot. I forgot to hit my own floor," I heard him say.

And just like that, the elevator doors closed; him on one side and me on the other. I exhaled the biggest sigh of disappointment ever. The fantasy was over. It was back to business, and reality, as usual.

"Damn," I scolded myself. I wish I knew what floor he was getting off on. But I didn't let that discourage me. If it was meant for me and Dr. Cannon to be, then we would definitely connect. For now, though, I had a patient to see and I couldn't let visions of Dr. McHottie sidetrack me.

I began the second half of my day with continuous thoughts of Dr. Cannon reflecting in my mind as I was making rounds from room to room. I did not foresee any deliveries for the remainder of my shift. I had the opportunity to sit back, rewind, and replay the image of Dr. Cannon in my mind.

Before I knew it, my day came and went. Some people didn't have as much action take place in a week of their life as I did in a single day. As full as my day had been, it was time to put away the scrubs and hit the road.

I never got the opportunity to hit Tasha up and inquire about Dr. Cannon. Just thinking about that man made me tingle between my thighs. I envisioned him taking me in that elevator, pressing me up against the wall, and doing all kinds of dirty little things to me. As we rode the elevator, I would ride him.

It was times like this that made me feel as though I was living a double life. My image during the day was that of a professional, loving doctor who handled herself with finesse and class. That was the day version of me, the one I projected anyway; my representative so to speak. But come night, I was footloose and fancy free. I enjoyed having fun and enjoying myself . . . and the opposite sex if I was lucky.

My hormones always seemed to take complete control. My body constantly desired endless pleasure. I loved the opportunity to explore new pastures. I would much rather enjoy sexual pleasure than to eat at a five star restaurant. I was once told by my friend and colleague, Tracy, who worked part-time at the hospital, that I needed psychological counseling because of my sexual appetite. Well, if I had things my way, Dr. Cannon would one day soon end up on my menu. Who knew? Maybe he'd even end up being my main course. I didn't know when and I didn't know where, but I felt it in my bones that Dr. Cannon and I would meet again.

Chapter 4

I was dressed to kill; hair, nails, and makeup on point. I had planned to meet up with Tracy at Daiwa Sushi, however, the weather dictated an alternate agenda. It was raining cats and dogs, and their owners too! The thunderstorm mixed with the colorful lightening was massive. The poor weather conditions shifted my entire mood. I had looked out of my window after hearing a loud cracking sound from Mother Nature, only to find a rainstorm in full effect. Prior to that I'd been ready to go out and enjoy the nightlife.

I had on my one-piece khaki jumper that one would have thought had been made just for me. It complemented my thick waist and even thicker hips. The four inch nude patent leather pumps I was wearing boosted me up from the five feet, six inches that I already stood in height. But even after staring out of the window momentarily and watching the raindrops hit the pavement like grenades being shot over from Korea, my rocking appearance could not compete with the solemn laziness that overtook my entire being.

Hopeful, I waited for a few minutes before making my final call as to whether to stay in for the evening. I'd hate for all my efforts to look so good go to waste, so I at least wanted to give the rain time to let up. It never did. Not after a half hour

. . . not even after an hour. The rain clouds had opened up and looked as if they had no plans of closing anytime soon. My mind was made up; Mother Nature prevailed. I went from being a hot potato ready to hit the streets, to a couch potato.

Now for the worst part of it all, I'd have to tell Tracy that I was not coming out in this mess. I didn't want to have to call her up, as we'd both been looking forward to our little outing all week. Tasha was scheduled to work this weekend, so she couldn't join us.

I couldn't prolong it any longer. I grabbed my cell phone and went to dial Tracy's number, but it started ringing before I could even dial.

"Fuck," I mumbled under my breath after looking at the caller ID screen. It was Tracy. I'd really wanted to call her before she had the chance to call me. But maybe I'd be in luck and she was calling me to cancel our plans.

"Hey," I said into the phone. I was trying to sound neutral so that she couldn't detect my mood.

"What up, chick? You ready to do this?"

The way she spoke into the phone all happy-go-lucky, I could tell she was ready to go kick it. She had no intentions of cancelling our little outing. That made having to tell her that I was bailing on her that much harder. Not wanting to disappoint her couldn't keep me from taking off my clothes. My mind was made up as I began slipping out of my clothes as I cradled the phone between my ear and shoulder.

"Hey, girl. I'm over here waiting on you," she said. "I thought you said you were coming at around eight. It's almost nine. What's up?" She didn't sound irritated, simply ready to go.

"I don't know what's up, but I know what's coming down, this rain. And I was all dressed and ready to go too."

"What do you mean *was*?" she said, most of her chipperness

gone at this point.

"You know how rain makes some folks want to stay inside? Well, I'm one of those folks."

"Girl, I know you are not about to flake out on me," Tracy said. "I am fully dressed, face beat, sitting here waiting on you. I didn't eat all damn day making sure I could fit into this little black dress minus a FUPA. Are you serious right now?"

FUPA stood for Fat Upper Pubic Area, of which Tracy did not have. Skinny girls killed me thinking they were fat.

Hearing Tracy go on her rant made me feel bad. To make it worse, I was supposed to be driving tonight. The arrangement was that I was going to scoop Tracy up at her place. Reason being, for one, she lived on the way to the restaurant. For two, she'd told her sister who lived with her that she could use her car since I was going to be the one driving. Seeming I was her only means of transportation, I could understand her not being a happy camper.

"I just got my hair done yesterday. I'm not about to try to come out and have that moisture ruin my bone straight, flat ironed do," I said. "So can we pleassseee take a rain check, literally?" I chuckled at the little joke I'd made to try and lighten the mood.

"I ain't trying to be out with somebody who doesn't want to be out. That ain't no fun, so just forget it."

"You mad?" I said in a whiny tone, knowing the answer.

"Whatever, Denise. Bye!"

The next thing I heard was a click in my ear. She was mad now, but I'd give her a couple days to cool off. Then I'd invite her out for sushi again. This time it would be my treat. That would help her get over it.

Within an hour after our call, she was over it. She'd sent me a text that read: Good you kept your rusty butt home. My sister brought my car back and I went on by myself. I have been in the company of a new potential boo. Three would have been a crowd. So now!

All I could do was smile. That girl had been bound and determined to go out and be seen. She wasn't about to let this one monkey stop her show. I was happy for her, though. Tracy was an extrovert. She didn't mind going places and doing things by herself. She wouldn't be by herself for long. The girl had never met a stranger in her life.

Tracy and I had shared a twenty year friendship. She was the one who had told me about Sentara. We'd met in Anatomy and Physiology class during undergraduate studies. I guess I just told my age. But hey, I'm a proud forty-something. And I look damn good! Tracy looked good as well. Our black didn't crack. Upon graduation, I went on to become an Obstetrician, of course, while Tracy became a Pediatrician.

Our dream was to someday open the first all-Black female multidisciplinary group in the suburbs of Norfolk. That was part of my plan I mentioned earlier about running my own practice. Our dream still had potential; it's just that we were missing the third link. We needed a well-respected female Gynecologist to fill the gap. But from the sounds of things, a woman was the last thing on Tracy's mind. It sounded like she was about to get lucky.

I decided that since I was staying home, that didn't mean I couldn't enjoy good libations, so I hugged up with my favorite liquor, Vodka. This smooth tasting Cîroc became my new plan for the evening. You know I had to set the mood as well. I dimmed the lights in the kitchen, turned on the sounds, and began mellowing out to the beat of Maxwell's "Pretty Wings."

I bypassed the dining room, swaying to the music, and made my way to the living room where I claimed a small section of the couch. My home had an open concept; one room led me right into the next. It often reminded me of an oversized efficiency apartment, the kind where some people separate sections of the room with those three-part room dividers.

After snuggling up on the couch and nodding my head to one of the sexiest voices on wax, vinyl, or whatever today's technology used to provide the sound of music, I fell into an alcohol induced sleep. My workday was still playing an active role in my mind even as I slept. Thoughts of some of my patients came to pass, especially the young ones who seemed like they were starting off on the wrong foot in life by becoming teenage parents. But they were so rumbustious and naïve, thinking this was the way of life, mainly because it had been the life of many generations before them. They were much like those from my hometown of Aliquippa. I began reminiscing about my own teenage years.

It was another fall day in early October of my senior year. Everyone was at the stadium cheering on the Aliquippa Quips football team. The band was under the direction of Mr. Romeo and the drum major. Cheerleaders and pom-pom girls were all dressed in red and black. The field was muddy and the temperature varied as the season progressed. I, along with the rest of the clarinet and flute section, marched in unison to the sounds of Michael Jackson's "Beat It."

Even though she had long since graduated, this last game made me think of Tasha. I remember when she performed for the final time her senior year. She went out with a bang. This would be my last and final time marching on the home field. Like Tasha, I had to kill it.

My steps were precise, my posture admirable, and I played that clarinet gracefully just as Tasha and I used to do together on the last regular season game. We always showed out because once the regular season came to an end, we were treated with celebrity status.

The audience involvement was electrifying as they rocked to the tunes as well, which made me that much more pumped up. The drum major added his special effects until the very end of the halftime show. Everyone was on their feet chanting, "Let's go Quips! Let's go Quips!"

The team was on fire. The Quips were playoff bound with a 12-0 record, ranking number one in their division. The Fighting Quips were competing for the title of WPIAL, which was the Western Pennsylvania Interscholastic Athletic Association, championship. It was a sure ride to Three Rivers Stadium, that's if they could break out of the 17-17 tie against the Beaver Falls Tigers, their rival since forever. The excitement in the stadium was explosive as the wide receiver ran a seventy yard interception to score the winning touchdown.

That night we all headed to Avenue Café to celebrate. Most of our parents extended our curfews in honor of the win. Come Saturday morning, I was dog tired. I was in and out of sleep when I overheard my sister and mother's conversation about who was going to wake me up to come eat breakfast. The smell of blueberry muffins had already made their way into my bedroom and into my nostrils. Growing up, my mother's blueberry muffins with bacon on the side was my favorite breakfast. I don't care how tired I was, I was not going to miss gobbling some down.

"I'm awake. No one has to wake me up," I yelled in a groggy tone.

My sister replied, "Mom made your favorite muffins, come and get some."

I got out of bed, headed into the bathroom for my morning visit, then downstairs I went.

They had the table decorated with balloons, muffins, bacon, and OJ. Mom was standing at the head of the table looking all sheepish with envelopes in her hand.

I sat down at the table. My sister wore a huge grin on her face as my mother just stood there.

"What?" I asked. "What's going on with you two?" I looked from my sister to my mother. Finally, my mother handed me the envelopes she held in her hand.

"What's this?" I asked, noticing that my mother's facial expression was that of pure admiration.

I looked down at the envelopes and my heart skipped a beat when I realized they were letters from three out of the four colleges I had applied to. So many thoughts began to bombard my mind. What if I didn't get into any of the schools? What if I got into all of them? Which one would I choose to attend? This was really a high point in my life; a seventeen year old with so many decisions to make. Whatever decisions I decided to make, I knew a promising future was ahead.

I was in the top five percent of my graduating class. Even though I had a pretty good chance of getting into one, if not all of the schools I was interested in attending, the military appeared as appealing as a four year university.

I had to be smart in my choices. Getting into a university was one thing, but paying the tuition was something totally different. I'd applied for grants and scholarships, but if those didn't come through, I was screwed. We lived in the projects for crying out loud. Nobody had set any money aside for college tuition.

The Air Force was offering to pay my full tuition in exchange for me signing up for at least two tours of duty as an officer. Two tours would mean a total of eight years. I figured I could do that with one eye open and one eye closed. That wasn't an easy sell to my mother though.

"Niecy, wouldn't it be much better to enter the military with a college degree versus going in straight out of high school?" my mother had asked.

I looked into what my mother was saying a little more. I learned that if I would elect to go straight in the Air Force after high school, I would be an enlisted soldier/noncommissioned officer without a four year degree. If I obtained the under graduate degree prior to entering the military, I would be a commissioned officer. The pay would be double and my doctoral studies would be free. Talk about mother knows best.

I really didn't care how I did it or what I had to do to achieve my goals, which was to become a successful physician. I wanted a prestigious profession that guaranteed an income that would keep me off government assistance in any shape or form, including government housing. I'd looked into both the medical and legal field. STEM, Science, Technology,

Engineering and Math, wasn't as popular back then as it is in today's world of education. As it turned out, medicine would become my passion. It was a field that would provide me the opportunity to help others while also giving me a feeling of accomplishment.

The military provided the training without thousands of dollars in loans to repay. The decision to go to OSU, one of the schools that accepted me, then into the Airforce was decided with the mature guidance of my mother.

"Shit!" I blurted out after the ringing phone pulled me from my dream, plus startled me a little. *Headache.* Cîroc and being woken up out of my sleep equaled a throbbing headache.

With my hand on my forehead and my eyes squinted, I looked at my caller ID. I could have been knocked over with a feather when I saw "Mommy" on the screen. I had dreamed my mother up.

I leaned over to pick up the phone while I yawned. "Hey, Ma."

There was not a greeting, hello, or anything. She got straight to the point. "That boy you were in the service with died," my mom said, wasting no time at all at getting to the purpose of her call. "He was your age and left three little babies behind. They say he just dropped dead in his bathroom coming out of the shower."

First, I had to wriggle myself out of my drunken stupor and allow the words my mom was rattling off without even taking a breath to register in my head. "Mom, who is 'that boy' you are talking about?" I asked. "I was half sleep and hardly heard a word you said." All of a sudden I thought my bladder was going to burst. I looked on the table at the half empty bottle of Cîroc and my half-filled glass. I had drunk that shit like it was wine. No wonder I was about to pee my pants. "Look, Ma, let me call you right back."

"Hurry up," she said, "so I can finish telling you about him."

"Okay, I will. I promise."

I hung up that phone and barely made it to the toilet in time. Pee had actually begun to trickle out. I was doing a wiggle dance upon entering the bathroom. I made it before the real explosion erupted. As I relieved myself, I pondered over who the heck my mother was trying to tell me had passed away. If I recalled correctly, she said I'd been in the service with him and that he was my age. That was pretty young to die. He'd hardly had a chance to live life.

That made me start thinking about several deployments. There had been France, Spain, Germany, Italy, Egypt, and Saudi Arabia, not to mention multiple statewide tours where I had run into high school classmates from Aliquippa. I could not pinpoint who exactly my mother was talking about, and I wasn't about to wrack my brain trying to figure it out. I was going to preserve the little bit of my buzz I had left.

I washed my hands and this time headed to my bedroom. As I climbed in my bed, my mom having brought up the military began to make me think about my years of service.

When I retired from the USAF, I had twenty years of service under my belt. An LTC's, Lt. Colonel, retirement pay was not bad, but the love of assisting in childbirth wouldn't allow me to retire from the profession altogether. I was not about to allow my MD degree to sit and collect dust, besides, I was only in my early forties. I still had a great future ahead of me. So even though I decided to call it quits and retire from the military, being a doctor was not something I was ready to give up doing.

Once I received the offer letter from Sentara, I was more determined than ever to head to the States with or without my family. When I say family, no, I'm not talking about my mom, sister, brother, or anything like that. I'm talking about my immediate family; daughter and husband.

Not only did I get a post doctorate degree while in the military, but I got pregnant as well. My second year of service I gave birth to my only child, my daughter Kendra. I know, right! Who would have thought that I was somebody's mama? From the outside looking in I appeared to be this carefree, single woman with no kids. But that's because my baby girl was currently living with her dad in Rhein-Main, Germany. The plan had always been for Kendra to stay with him until school was out, and then move back to the States with me. The base they lived on was located near the city of Frankfurt, Germany. I'd lived there for one tour of duty.

Kendra's father, Dwayne, decided it would be best for Kendra to complete her school year overseas. He thought that was best for a six year old child, versus forcing her to make such a major transition in the middle of the school semester. Me hanging around waiting for Kendra to finish school was not an option. I couldn't get out of Germany fast enough, which was the reason for my abrupt departure.

Our relationship was not close; Dwayne's and mine of course, because my relationship with my daughter was everything. Me and little mama were tight. Although Dwayne and I had vowed to be husband and wife only a year before Kendra was born, as the marriage went on, our commitment seemed more of a business arrangement than a union. The business was on the verge of emotional bankruptcy, a chapter 11. I had to get out of dodge before I witnessed it transition to a chapter 13, finding ourselves with nothing left to give. At least this way even though we might not have had anything to give to one another emotionally, we still had much to offer our child.

I had retired from the Air Force and began my new job

here in Norfolk all within the same month. I did not even let the dust settle under my feet before transitioning from military to civilian life. The transition was not that complex professionally. The slight difference involved new staff and peers, learning a new computer system and paper work, as well as wearing scrubs as opposed to a military uniform.

It was hard to believe I was married. Needless to say, these days I didn't feel married and I damn sure didn't act married. Although so many women out there would have loved to be married to a doctor—Dr. Dwayne Simpson—I wasn't one of them. There was a time, though, when it was just the opposite.

Dwayne was my first love. He happened to be my preceptor during my Gynecology rotation at Langley Air Force Base in Hampton, Virginia. He was a Captain at the time. Life with Dwayne was exciting and great. Dwayne was drop-dead gorgeous, and when I'd met him he was a divorced father of a teenage son. His ex-wife and son were living in the Midwest at the time of our marriage. His son had visited a couple times before starting college. His son ended up going to study abroad, landing a crazy paying job over in Japan. The last I heard the ex-wife, LaDonna, was still living somewhere in the Midwest. She'd managed to stick her claws into another doctor. With the son being grown, there was definitely no reason to keep up with the ex-wife, especially when I'd become her replacement. Yes, once upon a time I'd been proud to stand side by side with the then Medical Director of Gynecological services.

I had truly loved that man unconditionally. He helped bring out the best in me, not to mention the extra pointers and extra credit he provided to help pass me along in class. Don't get it twisted; in no way, shape, or form had I been using Dwayne. I really loved that man. I loved what he did to me, not for me. So what I was the teacher's pet so to speak.

That didn't mean it was all taking and no giving on my part. Trust me when I say I gave a lot, so it was an even exchange as far as I was concerned. After all, pussy cannot be returned. Once it's gone, it's gone. I just thought I'd never see the day where I'd be saying that about our marriage.

Chapter 5

I was beginning to fall into the old Monday through Friday workday slump. This poverty-stricken work environment was beginning to overpower me. Perhaps Sentara was not the hospital for me after all. It offered a boatload of experience with the deliveries and high-risk pregnancies, but the clientele left little to be desired.

It was my entire fault for accepting the first position that was offered to me. Using it as a way to separate myself from Dwayne—my marriage altogether—I did not explore my options, or maybe even my worth. I'd applied for several jobs in various states in the US. The job offer from Sentara was the bird in the hand as far as I was concerned; the bird that would fly me away from my miserable marriage. Besides, at that point in time, my life was spiraling downward. My marriage was on the rocks and still is for that matter. My child had been in and out of the hospital for months, undiagnosed with persistent pain, recurring infections, and nausea. We had no family near to reach out to.

Kendra was eventually diagnosed with Sickle Cell Anemia. As a mother, I would do anything in exchange for a cure for such a dreadful disease. Sickle Cell Anemia was no joke. One in every six hundred African Americans was diagnosed with the disorder. Sickle Cell Anemia could lead to renal failure. It could also be fatal. I could only imagine the pain felt when regular banana shaped red blood cells changed shapes, causing it difficult for blood to circulate through the body. This caused such a severe pain, which was unbearable for a mother to watch their child go through. The pain was an indication of an onset of the Sickle Cell Crisis.

I'm glad to say that Kendra eventually got better, but unfortunately my marriage didn't.

I now realize that I made a hasty decision in accepting the job here in Norfolk; nonetheless, there was no going backward. I had done my time at Sentara, and as a result, I had clinically diagnosed myself with "Ghetto Burnout." My definition of Ghetto Burnout was watching generations of females repeating the actions of their preceding unwed mothers, sisters, cousins, and aunts who had struggled to raise children alone.

Even though I had not completed the two-year term of my current contract with the hospital, on the low, I'd already begun looking for an alternate employment opportunity out of state. I didn't even care about the breach of contract clause in my employment contract with Sentara. It clearly stated that an employee must repay the entire signing bonus should he/she decide to terminate the contract prematurely for whatever reason. In my case, that would be $10,000, which was a fair exchange for a little happiness.

I was considering North Carolina, Florida, or Ohio as places to relocate. I was somewhat familiar with Ohio, after all, I had resided in Columbus during my undergraduate studies at The Ohio State University. I would not have minded going back to the capital city, but Columbus didn't have any positions that sparked my interest. However, Cleveland did.

I'd searched for vacant positions in the surrounding Cleveland area until I found the perfect fit for me. The job was at Rainbow Babies & Children's Hospital. It was straight

Monday through Friday with rotating weekends, which meant I only had to work one weekend every six weeks. Another plus was that the hospital was located in a middle-upper class neighborhood. I think that if perhaps I could up my game by dealing with folks who worked for a living like me, I would begin to appreciate not only my job, but the patients I served. Let's just face it; servicing the undeserved and underprivileged was not my plight in life. That's why I thought working at Rainbow versus Sentara would be better for me.

I'd applied to Rainbow online two weeks ago, and within a few days I had received an email acknowledging receipt of my application. A POC, Point of Contact, was assigned to me. I then began to forward all requested documents in a timely manner. I sent a copy of my medical license, a copy of my DEA license, a copy of my board certification, and a copy of my CV, aka, Curriculum Vitae. A CV is a comprehensive document of a person's past education, competencies, and professional development. It's very similar to that of a resume. The only difference is that a resume is not as detail oriented. I came to an obstacle when I had to provide three references; one professional and two personal. The personal references were not a problem. It was the professional reference that halted my progress.

In the world of medicine, the professional reference should be someone who can vouch for at least the past two years of an applicant's employment. I hadn't even been employed at Sentara a year, therefore I could not ask any of my colleagues there. Not only that, but I didn't want them to get wind that I was job hunting. Sometimes when an employer learned that an employee was seeking work elsewhere, they'd find a reason to let them go before they quit. I did not want such a blemish on my work record.

As I sat and pondered, I concluded that only one person

knew my strengths and weaknesses. I learned all of my medical skills from him. My work ethic was nothing but a replica of his own. So what other option did I have but to pick up the phone and call him?

I picked up the phone three times. I'd hung up twice before even dialing all of the digits of the phone number on the third time. It was certainly a mental struggle. We didn't really communicate verbally; that was always so awkward. But what the hell? On that third go 'round I dialed each number and allowed it to ring. My heart nearly dropped when he picked up. I swallowed hard and then spoke.

"Hello, Dwayne." I didn't even give him a chance to return the greeting. Before I lost my courage, I had to get out what I had called to ask him. "I have been considering another position," I told him, making sure I didn't dare let the cat out of the bag that the position was not at Sentara Hospital. He didn't need to know all that just yet. "I have been asked to forward references. Would you be opposed to being a professional reference for me?" I let it all out, not allowing any interruptions between words.

This question must have sparked a pack of firecrackers in his head. He began popping off a whole crap load of questions. "Why do you need a professional reference? Are you moving? Are you changing jobs? What is going on?"

"I just want a change is all," I said.

"Speaking of change," he said. "You know my current enlistment is ending. I was thinking that perhaps Kendra and I could return to the States together."

"Instead of you just sending Kendra alone?" I quickly injected. I had to make sure I was hearing him correctly. Not only that, but even if he and Kendra did come together, where the hell was his ass going to sleep? We were married, but more like married strangers. I didn't need any strangers sleeping in my bed.

"I was, uh, kind of thinking about us, if we could maybe try to give our marriage one more chance to survive." Dwayne, who usually spit out whatever was on his mind, seemed to be stammering.

Meanwhile, my mind was stumped. I guess I knew where he planned on sleeping. This was not how I thought this conversation was going to go. This conversation was supposed to be about me, and here he went making it about us. This was totally coming out of left field. There hadn't been an *us* when it came to Dwayne and me in a long time. Even when we were living under the same roof together *we* didn't feel like an *us*. I was ready and able to accept Kendra with open arms. Oh how I had missed her. But Dwayne? That was another story.

What had changed in our lives and in his mind—other than our separate living arrangements many, many miles apart—to make him want to try to work things out? Although it was a given, it was unspoken that when I left Germany, I was leaving our marriage. Keeping it one hundred, I'd been in the VA living like a single woman . . . and I' grown to like the way it felt.

Why was it imperative for us to make a mends at this point in our estranged marriage? Our relationship had grown farther and farther apart the more we were under the same roof. The union appeared to be nothing more than a business partnership, with Kendra being the product of our investment.

"Dee, I realize things were and are not great for us," Dwayne said, "but I am willing to put my all, one hundred percent, into restoring a new beginning for us if you will have me again. We are getting older and Kendra is growing up. She needs to recognize her parents can work this marriage out together." His voice continued to echo words that, in my ears, began running together without meaning.

What he was saying made sense, but again, only for business purposes; the business of raising our child. But in all his reasons for us to get back together, he said nothing about love. I guess that's why Tina wrote the infamous words, "What's love got to do with it?" Clearly, in Dwayne's mind, it had nothing to do with it . . . nothing to do with *us*.

In between every pause he took, awaiting a reply from me, I simply continued to say, "Oh, okay, we will see." My voice did not get higher or lower during the conversation. The pitch remained the same, monotone. I was emotionally frozen, so my mouth was operating on autopilot.

Thank goodness it was the weekend. This particular weekend I was on-call status. I only had to report to the hospital in an emergency situation. Hopefully there would be no emergency, because all I was going to be able to focus on was the bomb Dwayne had dropped by way of asking me to give our marriage another shot. His single question gave birth to many more in my mind. My brain was going to be spinning. I'd need all weekend and my liquid bestie, Cîroc, to get right by Monday.

"Well, what do you say?" Dwayne asked. "All you've been saying is, 'Oh, okay.' Does that mean you are okay with us giving our marriage a try, or are you just saying 'Oh, okay' because you hear what I'm saying?"

Damn it! Now he wanted me to be specific in my response. But I couldn't. I honestly didn't know what to say. So I said nothing.

"Look, why don't you give it some thought?" Dwayne said, interrupting the silence.

I did not respond with a yes, nor did I respond with a no. I had to weigh my options, my pros and cons. Would Dwayne and I truly work on our marriage, or would it basically be us relocating our place of doing business co-parenting?

Was I ready to open my heart again for a relationship that had long been closed? Was it fair to our daughter that two grown ass adults could not get it together? Did she deserve to continue to witness our humdrum and stale interactions? Did she deserve to be escorted to her school functions by whichever one of us was on parent duty for the day, instead of all three of us attending as a family unit? The same way we had shifts working in the hospital, Dwayne and I had shifts in the home and when it came to Kendra.

Everything was so boring and predictable with Dwayne. If I decided to work it out with him, would I be settling instead of moving forward with what could be a fun and exciting life? During my stint here in Virginia, I'd gotten a little taste of what it felt like to be alive. With each question I asked myself, the more afraid I became of the answers. But what was I afraid of? I was Denise Simpson, the fearless one; never letting anything stop me. Never letting anything get in my way. Somehow my emotions, after all these years, were deciding that they wanted to have a say in what I did with my life. I wasn't used to that.

Multiple questions continued to invade my thought process. They continued just like the constant flow of a stream in a river. I could feel a headache emerging. I needed time to think, but I would soon learn that time was something Dwayne was not going to give me.

He remained persistent in calling me periodically throughout the entire weekend. His mind must have been wandering all over the place too. My calling him to be a reference must have struck a chord with him, the *This-marriage-is-really-over* chord. The *she's-going-to-keep-moving-on-in-life-without-me* chord. It definitely lit some kind of fire in him. Before this weekend, I could count on one hand how many times

Dwayne and I talked in a month's time. Although Kendra and I spoke daily, Dwayne and I seldom corresponded verbally. We would email or text from time to time with updates on Kendra's school performance and medical appointments.

Why all of a sudden was his desire for us to reunite so strong? There had to be a hidden agenda. There had to be something that triggered his desperate actions other than me calling him up to be a reference. But perhaps this would all simply die down as time passed.

Come Sunday night, when I spoke with Kendra, I could tell by what she said to me that Dwayne had been taking this reuniting thing serious.

"Mommy, Daddy told me that we were moving to Virginia to be with you when school is out. I can't wait to see you, hug, love, and give you lots and lots of smooches."

I was numb. I never wanted to be a disappointment to my baby girl. God knows I have had my fair share of lonely childhood memories growing up without a father. I was so very torn inside, primarily because Kendra had a loving relationship with her father, something that I never experienced. Yet, on the other hand, I did not want her to grow up in an unhealthy, loveless, and unaffectionate environment, sensing that her parents were not in love. As the old folks say; staying together for the kids. I didn't want to be the person to teach her that it's okay to forego true happiness. But that's exactly what I'd been doing.

I was willing to bet the farm that Dwayne had told Kendra those things on purpose in order to persuade me to give in. He wasn't slick. I'd expressed to Dwayne before leaving Germany how guilty I felt leaving Kendra behind. He made me feel better by helping me to realize that it was best for her to finish school there. I felt even better when we discussed it with Kendra and she preferred to stay at a school with her friends and then come live with me. Whatever made Kendra happy I was always willing to do it, even if it made me not so happy. Dwayne was well aware that letting my baby girl down was the last thing I ever wanted to do. It was the one thing I wouldn't do.

With that final thought, I said to Kendra, "Me too baby, me too." Before I knew it, my neutral stand had turned into a yes.

Kendra and I said our goodnights, being silly and telling each other we loved one another more than the moon and back. Dwayne then got on the phone.

"Denise, I can't wait for us to be back together as a family." Clearly he had been standing there listening to Kendra's and my conversation. I could hear the sound of victory in his voice. He'd won with his sneaky move of using Kendra to fully persuade me. "This is perfect timing. It's the best gift I could ever receive."

Ooooh, I could picture him wearing a smirk that if I'd been standing in front of him, I would have knocked off his face. We were not even back in each other's presence yet and I was already thinking about doing him bodily harm. Had I made one of the biggest mistakes in my life by agreeing to be with Dwayne . . . again?

"I love you," were his next words that floated through the phone receiver and into my ear.

After I was able to find my voice that had been lost in a whirlwind of shock, my reply was a simple, "Good night," and then I ended the call.

I stared at my phone. What in the hell had just happened? I had not heard those three words out of his mouth intended for my ears in over a year. Why now—as I was mentally building up the confidence to raise and take care of Kendra as a single parent—did he want to reconcile things?

If I were to give our marriage another try, my flowery dream of Dr. Cannon would not blossom into reality. The mysterious RC would have certainly been a breath of fresh air. Like they say, or like they should say, nothing helps a woman get over old dick like new dick, and I'd planned on Dr. Cannon helping me get over my broken marriage.

The plan was to continue investigating the unknowns about the fine doctor. Hell, in my mind I had already cheated with him during that elevator ride. In my colorful imagination, the man was playing an active role as my leading man. He was my excuse, my reason to strongly not consider getting back with Dwayne, that and the fact I wasn't in love with Dwayne anymore. I loved Dwayne, and it was possible that I could fall back in love with him. Anything was possible. But it was going to be pretty difficult if my thoughts of Dwayne were competing with thoughts of Dr. Cannon, a man I didn't even know, which brought a whole other set of questions to mind.

"What if Dr. Cannon is married?" I asked myself. I then frowned and said, "What if he is gay?"

Among other things, I couldn't help but wonder what if he did not find me attractive. After all, I didn't see him jumping up and down trying to get my phone number or anything. But then again, he didn't seem like the aggressive type. No, he was one of those smooth, laid back type of guys.

My mind shifted from Dr. Cannon to my husband. What if Dwayne was really going to give our marriage his all this time? What if the grass was not greener on the other side with Dr. Cannon? What if? What if? Ughhh!

I didn't even want to think about this day anymore. I'd deal with it tomorrow. But tomorrow wasn't promised, so I had to make sure my todays on Earth were happy and fulfilling. The question was whether or not they would be most fulfilling with or without Dwayne.

Chapter 6

I arrived to the hospital Monday morning eight minutes prior to the start of my shift. I was so proud of myself for making it on time, considering I hadn't gotten much sleep over the weekend. The whole Dwayne situation had me tossing and turning every time I tried to lie down and close my eyes.

I called into the nursing station to inform the staff that I was in-house, and to call me on my office line once the first patient arrived. There were no scheduled deliveries via C-Section or anything like that. But babies came when they got good and ready, so no telling how the day would pan out.

I decided to go to my office to read over my emails. There were only five messages in my inbox. Whew! No crazy questions from patients. Thank you, Jesus!

The first two emails were from Dwayne. "Damn," I mumbled under my breath. "Hadn't he said enough with all the phone calls this weekend?" I didn't immediately crack open his email, as I scrolled to see who the others were from. Two of the remaining emails were from the Cleveland POC, while the last one was from Tasha.

Dwayne's first email had "SURPRISE/UPDATE" written in the subject line. I opened and read it. He was informing me that his Air Force separation date was this coming Friday. He was about to begin processing out of the base and expected to be back into the States within a month. He was officially done with his service to our great country, and travel arrangements were in the works. He still had thirty vacation days left on the books. He wouldn't lose them though. The military would allow him those thirty days to tie up any loose ends in preparation for any type of relocation or move.

My stomach started to churn, like how a belly does when it's uneasy. This was all happening way sooner than I had expected, which explained Dwayne's sense of urgency in us getting back together all of a sudden. He didn't want to try to ease back into things by dating or talking more on the phone; simply reconnecting. Nope! He wanted to dive in head first by moving back in together.

I clicked open one of the other emails from Dwayne, which had "HAPPY ANNIVERSARY" in the subject line. I was an emotional wreck. Today was our anniversary. The fact that the date Dwayne and I joined as one had escaped my mind should have spoken volumes. Today was just another day on my desk calendar. Last year we were under the same roof for our anniversary and didn't as much as say the words "Happy Anniversary" to one another, let alone go out to dinner or exchange gifts.

"Gift," I mumbled under my breath and then thought back to something Dwayne had said during one of our phone calls.

"This is perfect timing. It's the best gift I could ever receive."

Before, it had gone right over my head. Now I knew exactly what he'd meant by that statement.

The fact that Dwayne was acknowledging the date meant that at least he was trying.

I looked down at the time on the bottom of the computer screen. It was already fifteen minutes past the hour and I had not heard from the nurses. I checked the computer registration menu. The first patient was marked a "NO SHOW." The patient after that had cancelled and rescheduled. Hell, this was the one day I could have been late to work. I wouldn't have missed a thing.

With at least thirty more minutes to spare, I continued opening emails. My heart skipped a beat when the email from the hospital in Cleveland informed me that they wanted me to fly in for an interview. I couldn't stop smiling at the prospect of me getting the job. Somehow in between Dwayne's phone calls to me, he did manage to prepare a reference letter that I had emailed to Cleveland just yesterday afternoon. It was actually the same reference letter he'd prepared for my job here at Sentara. He'd tweaked it some, which is why it had taken very little effort for him to get it to me. They must have cracked open that email first thing this morning and been pretty impressed with all the things Dwayne had to say about me; that combined with my past work history and experience. They might not have even read Dwayne's reference letter. They could have been merely waiting on me to supply them with everything on their list of requirements to complete the application.

My initial excitement and smile quickly faded. I let out a grunt and buried my face in the palm of each hand. This was good news. This was great news, but the timing of it was blowing my mind.

My daughter and husband would be joining me in Virginia; the exact date I didn't yet know. But with my luck, if I agreed to fly out to Cleveland, it would be the same date Dwayne and Kendra would be flying into Virginia. It wouldn't be a good start if I were in Cleveland and not here to greet them. I suppose it would be an even worse start if they arrived in Virginia, I'd gotten the job at Rainbow, and was living in Cleveland!

No matter what kind of spin I put on things, it seemed inevitable that Dwayne and I were somehow going to end up right back in the same boat where we'd started. Only this time Kendra would be living with me and not him.

This job was an opportunity of a lifetime for me to start fresh career wise. My current position simply had not panned out to be what I had hoped it would. The independence and feeling like a boss chick was priceless, but dealing with the clientele I dealt with sometimes made it feel worthless. I felt unappreciated and a lack of respect for the initials behind my name. Folks who have been enabled all their life form a sense of entitlement and don't appreciate shit. Well damn it, I wanted to be appreciated.

I was being bombarded with far too many decisions at one time. I couldn't get my mind right long enough to even decide what I was going to do one way or the other. Now I could see how doctors ended up writing themselves a prescription. I was getting a splitting headache.

Life was such a rollercoaster ride, a journey that could result in a dead-end. The adventure of it all, though, was full of open and closed doors. It was the selection process of which door to choose that was the killer.

I was going to gamble with time to find out what cards I would be dealt. But in it all, I couldn't let my baby girl down. I had to stand strong in my 'yes.' I had to give this family thing a try for both her and my husband. If it didn't work out, at least I could honestly tell the judge that I'd tried.

My agenda was to move forward with giving our marriage another shot. I would also move forward with seeking employment in Cleveland as well. I had no idea how all of this was going to pan out. I had paid full price for my journey, now all I had to do was prepare for the ride.

***

The day began and ended uneventful at the hospital. I personally didn't have to make any deliveries, just routine GYN exams. The days following were exact repeats, which gave me too much time to think. But isn't that how life is? As the old folks would call it, the calm before the storm?

Dwayne, Kendra, and I had talked daily for the past three weeks. In only four more days we would all actually be in the same home once again as a family. I had already put in for a couple vacation days to spend time with them. I informed the POC in Cleveland that I was very much interested in the position. I explained the situation with Dwayne and Kendra arriving. To my delight, they were very understanding. They scheduled my interview far enough out so that I could spend time preparing for their arrival, plus spend a couple weeks helping them get settled in. That would give me at least two weeks to bond with my family and to also update Dwayne on the pending plans to relocate to another state. I had no idea how I was going to relay that to him. Even worse, I had no idea how he was going to respond.

I was certain he was not going to be thrilled, but the ball was in my court now; I was calling the shots. In my mind, even though Dwayne wrote an excellent reference that may have assisted me in obtaining the interview, he did not dig deeper regarding the aspects of the position I was being considered for. He wrote the wording and emailed it to me. I added the proper address and recipient, and then sent it to where it needed to go. All the while, I'm certain Dwayne was assuming it was for something local or right here at Sentara. After all, I hadn't been in Virginia an entire year yet. The last thing I'm sure he was thinking was that I planned on relocating to another state. It was going to be mind-blowing once the cat got out of the bag.

For the time being he was thrilled and completely satisfied

with my willingness to give this marriage another shot. He didn't want to rock the boat, and at this point, neither did I.

The day came when it was time to pick Dwayne and Kendra up from the airport. Needless to say, I had a sleepless night the previous night. The few glasses of Cîroc I'd drunk hadn't even put me in my usual tipsy stupor. I was just that anxious inside. My brain was on overload. I didn't even answer my phone when it rang. I did not want any company nor did I want any conversations with anyone. I could not shake the unsettling feeling I held in my stomach regarding reuniting with Dwayne.

"Jesus, take the wheel," I said to myself as I drove to the airport. I literally wanted Him to take the wheel before I ended up driving off a cliff as if death was better than what I was about to endure.

My cell phone rang. I grabbed it from the center console where I kept it while driving. I thought it might be Dwayne calling to tell me that their plane had landed. I realized I'd thought wrong once I looked at the screen.

"What up, chick?" I tried to sound cheery so that the caller wouldn't chew me out for not returning calls.

"What up my ass," Tasha spat through the phone.

No such luck. I hadn't talked to Tasha since we met up at her condo a couple weeks ago where I poured my heart out to her over drinks and pizza about my reunion with Dwayne.

"I called you like twice last night," Tasha said. "You didn't answer and you didn't return my call."

"I didn't get a message to call you back," I said, trying to pay close attention to the airport signs leading me to passenger pick-up.

"Don't play with me. You know you've seen that I've called you by now."

If Tasha had been in my face, I'm sure I would have seen

her rolling her eyes. Instead, I could only listen to her suck her teeth.

"Your fam in town yet?" Tasha's tone shifted at the mention of Kendra and Dwayne's arrival. Her voice was now laced with excitement. "I can't wait to meet my goddaughter."

I'm glad that at least one of us was excited. Yes, I was bursting at the seams with anticipation of seeing my daughter. My balloon of excitement would burst and deflate when thoughts of Dwayne would creep in.

"I'm at the airport now about to pick them up," I said to Tasha.

"That's why I was calling you last night, to see how you were feeling about everything. Having any second thoughts?"

"Seconds, thirds, fourths, and fifths." I let out a harrumph.

"I hear you. I don't know what I'd do if Clarence ever got right and wanted to get back together."

"Yes, you do," I was quick to say. "Your ass would be at the airport too."

We both let out a laugh.

"Shit!" I blurted out.

"What's wrong?" Tasha's voice filled with concern.

"I missed my turn. Oh well. I guess I'll just park and go inside and meet them, considering I'm headed toward short term parking."

"My bad. I didn't mean to distract you and make you get all discombobulated. I just wanted to make sure that you were good. Call me back when you get a minute and let me know how things are going."

"All right. Talk to you later."

"Bye."

I ended the call with Tasha, cussing myself out for missing my turn. Parking at the airport was a headache, not to mention expensive as hell.

Once I parked, I headed inside to the baggage claim area. In tow I had the teddy bear I'd purchased for my baby girl and a basket of treats filled with Kendra's favorite snacks and candy.

I walked into the airport and immediately dashed into the ladies' room. I didn't have to go extremely bad, but I didn't want to risk holding it until we got back home. Not with how shot my nerves were.

After handling my business, struggling to pee while securing all Kendra's stuff, I washed my hands and exited the bathroom. No sooner than I'd stepped out into the flow of foot traffic, I heard my name being spoken over the airport intercom.

"Denise Simpson, please meet your party at gate one in the baggage claim area. Denise Simpson, please meet your party at gate one."

What the…? I thought. Why hadn't Dwayne called me? Why blast my name all over the airport? That's when it hit me that he might have called me, but it would have been to no avail. I'd placed my phone back in the center console after talking to Tasha. I'd forgotten to grab it in the midst of carrying Kendra's gifts. That damn Tasha had gotten me all sidetracked.

I followed the instructions of the voice on the intercom and headed to gate one. The closer I got, the more my eyes darted in an attempt to spot Kendra and Dwayne. I spotted Kendra before Dwayne, only because of her bouncing ponytails as she came running toward me.

"Mommy, Mommy!" Kendra called out to me, opening her arms wide.

A huge smile spread across my face. I could already feel her arms wrapped around me. I placed the items I was carrying on the ground and then kneeled down to where I could receive her at her level.

Any feeling of nervousness and anxiousness evaporated as delight took over. Tears of joy began to flow down my face. I can honestly say that it was comparable to the way I felt the day I gave birth to such a perfect, beautiful little being.

"My baby girl," I said, opening my arms and allowing Kendra to throw herself into them. I hugged and kissed her over and over again all over her face and on her head. This was what people would call a Hallmark moment indeed. People were watching us, but I didn't care. In the beginning I didn't even notice. Kendra was my entire world, so for a moment there, it had felt like she and I were the only ones in the world. Oh but how I was quickly reminded that we weren't.

"Hey, lady. Save some of that sugar for me."

Who in the hell snatched the needle off the vinyl record that was playing my favorite song?

Dwayne's baritone voice suddenly reminded me that Kendra and I were not the only ones in the world or in the airport. She wasn't the only one in my life. I'd agreed to let Dwayne back in. So I suppose the least I could do was greet the man.

There he stood like a humble soldier awaiting his chance to be embraced.

"Dwayne." I stood up straight with my arms down to my side. I suppose the right thing to do would have been to spread them out to welcome a hug from Dwayne the same way I did for Kendra. It didn't come so easy though. Raising my arms felt like I was trying to lift fifty pound hand weights. It was a struggle, but I managed to open them and pull Dwayne in for a hug.

"Hey, you," I said. My chin rested on his shoulder as I stared upward. Talk about awkward.

He pulled his head back and kissed me on the lips, then

positioned himself fully into the hug. I think he could feel the awkwardness and the tension in my arms, because, as if he couldn't stand to put me through the discomfort any longer, he pulled out of the hug.

The hug and kiss was genuine, just awkward. I felt like a teenager kissing my childhood crush for the first time. You know that feeling you have when the big moment has arrived, but on the other hand there is an uncertainty that remains in the back of your mind? The physical attraction was still very strong. Dwayne was as fine, handsome, and clean-cut as ever. His facial features reminded me of Morris Chestnut, and his body too for that matter. He had smooth, chocolate skin and wide dreamy eyes. The combination of his broad shoulders and muscular biceps made it apparent he spent a great deal of time in the gym while in Germany. But there was still doubt. I shook away the thought and went on with the flow.

Dwayne looked me up and down. "You looking good."

I smiled and nodded, accepting the compliment.

After a few seconds of silence, Kendra's young self, sensing the uneasiness of it all, jumped in. "Is all that mine?" Her eyes were looking downward.

I'd forgotten about the gifts I'd placed on the ground. "What other princess could they possibly be for?" I said.

I was so relieved to now be giving Kendra my full attention again. "Here you go, baby." I handed Kendra her gifts as she fawned all over them.

"Well, we already have our luggage," Dwayne said, nodding toward his and Kendra's suitcases that were piled high on one of those carts.

They'd brought quite a bit of luggage, mostly clothing. He was having the remainder of their personal items shipped to Virginia along with his car. Since my place already had furniture, he sold everything he could from the home we once shared in Germany. He donated everything else to the Salvation Army.

"I'm parked in short-term parking," I said, leading the way.

As we walked to the parking garage, Dwayne and Kendra did all the talking. They were both upbeat, on full overdrive. Me, on the other hand, my bodily actions were that of neutral. I smiled and nodded; smiled and nodded. This was to show them that I'd heard them go on and on about not being able to wait to settle into their new place. But I wasn't listening. I was still in shock that this moment was actually transpiring.

Dwayne was speaking a mile a minute. "I'm sure the place is going to be nice. You've always had pretty good taste," he said. "After all, you picked me as a husband didn't you?"

Both Dwayne and Kendra laughed at his moment of conceit. I did my usual; smiled and nodded.

He continued on about this, that, and the other. I don't even think he stopped to breathe between words. "Once everything is kosher, I want us all to take a family vacation together. I know we've lived across the map, but we've never really taken the time to go somewhere just for fun and vacation like real families do."

"Oh, Daddy, I'd like that!" Kendra cheered.

It sounded as if the hubby had planned out our reunion and future life together with much thought. He continued to talk about plans for not only a family vacation, but for weekly family time together, a couples retreat for just him and me, and counseling for families that had been separated. He was on a mission to honor his martial vows.

By the time the car was loaded and we were all situated inside, he'd had the next two years of our lives all mapped out.

"I know it's been a long flight," he said over his shoulder

to Kendra, who sat in the backseat buckled up, "but I'm sure that doesn't keep you from wanting some good, old fashion DQ."

I looked in the rearview mirror and saw Kendra's eyebrows furrow in confusion.

"DQ stands for Dairy Queen," I told her.

"Yes, remember Daddy told you about it?" Dwayne said to Kendra. "The place that serves banana splits?"

Kendra's eyes lit up. "Dairy Queen! Oh yes." Kendra began bouncing up and down. "Can we, Mommy?"

"Yeah, can we, Mommy?" Dwayne chimed in, turning his attention to me.

The man knew ice cream was my favorite pickup. Ice cream and my baby girl; those two things made me happiest in the world. A good orgasm was a close runner up to ice cream though, but that would have been moving just a little too quickly for my pace. Dwayne and I had to warm up to each other. I needed to feel that intimate connection with him, that spark. And right now it wasn't there.

About fifteen minutes later we parked in the Dairy Queen's lot before exiting to get in line. Kendra leaned over the front seat and whispered in her father's ear. It was a kid whisper, though. The kind where those nearby could make out what she was saying.

"Don't forget the surprise you have to tell Mommy," Kendra said to her father.

"Okay," Dwayne said, replying in the same whisper tone that Kendra had spoken. He looked over at me and winked, knowing I'd heard their back and forth *whispering*. "I guess now would be as good a time as any to tell Mommy about the surprise."

Kendra could hardly contain herself as she continued to lean over the seat, now situated evenly between Dwayne and me.

He reached into his duffle bag he'd placed at his feet, pulled out an envelope, and extended it to me.

"What's that?" I asked, nodding toward the envelope.

"Open it up and find out," he said.

I stared at him for a moment, and then looked down at the envelope. I took it from his hands and opened it. I pulled the letter out from inside and began to read it.

My stomach dropped the same way it did the time Tasha and I rode that rollercoaster at an amusement park when we were in high school. I opened my mouth to speak, but nothing came out. I had nothing. No smile. No nod.

"Look, Daddy! Mommy is too happy to talk," Kendra exclaimed.

Kendra was half right. I couldn't talk, but it damn sure wasn't because I was happy. Confused, shocked, annoyed maybe, but not the least bit happy.

"So what do you think?" Dwayne waited for my reply in anticipation.

I pulled my eyes away from the letter and forced myself to push some words out of my mouth. "This is a surprise indeed." I really pushed myself by putting a smile on my lips, a crooked smile, but a smile no less.

Kendra scooted closer to me. "Not only will you and Daddy be living together again-"

"But we'll be working together too," Dwayne finished.

This son of a bitch was truly hell-bent on forcing me to reconcile with him at all cost.

The letter I held in my hand was the letter I was hoping to receive from the hospital in Cleveland after I nailed my interview. Dwayne had been offered a position at the same hospital I was currently employed at. Yep, Sentara Leigh Hospital. Stunned; that was another word to describe how I was feeling.

"Come on, so what do you think?" Dwayne asked with this huge grin on his face.

Every word I knew from the English language was stuck in my throat. Someone on the outside looking in would have thought I'd seen a ghost by my facial expression. I didn't want to show that I was not happy for him, but it was very difficult to hide my external feelings and appear to be excited. My immediate thought was why he wanted to work at Sentara. He had so many other options. He didn't have to work at all if he didn't want to. He could live off of the quarter million retirement from the military, pen a business, invest, or anything. Why was my option all of a sudden his?

"My contract for the hospital is only a year," he went on to explain excitedly, "but that's cool. This is just a stepping stone for two reasons."

Still speechless, I looked up at him.

"I want to see if things work out and our family wants to call Virginia home permanently."

He sat waiting on some type of verbal response from me, but I had nothing. My mind could not compute this news. I think he expected me to be overly excited, but my instinct was to be overly cautious.

"Isn't that great, Mommy?" Kendra said from the backseat. She was the one who now wanted me to verbalize how I felt regarding the *surprise*.

Trust and believe those two didn't want to hear what was really on my mind. This was our first day together. I did not want to spoil my baby girl's mood. But that damn Dwayne. All of this he was popping on me explained why he'd been in such a rush and so adamant about us reconciling; why he'd pushed so hard. He was full of surprises it seemed, and since his ass liked surprises so much, I figured it was the perfect opportunity for me to share one of my own.

I found my voice, clearing my throat while trying to sound calm. "Dwayne, although this was a kind gesture on your part, to want to work with me again, I'm not so sure we'll actually end up working together."

I wanted to pull my cell phone out and take a picture of the expression that now rested on his face. I'd wiped the smug grin right off of it. The hell with a camera, I should have videoed in real time his expression changing from "Oh yeah!" to "Oh shit!"

I continued on. "That reference you wrote me-"

"Yes, the one for a new position at Sentara." Although Dwayne intended for his words to form a simple statement, I could hear the questioning in his tone.

"Actually, it was for a position that I had applied for in Cleveland, Ohio. And partially thanks to your amazing reference I'm sure, I was informed that I am one of the four final selected candidates for the position. They wanted me to come to Cleveland for an interview a couple weeks ago, but I needed to prepare for you guys, so we arranged for me to go to Cleveland in a couple weeks."

I was actually pleased at how the whole interview schedule was working out. The POC notified me that they would interview the other three candidates first, and I'd be last. In my mind, it was beneficial to be able to leave the last and final impression out of all the candidates.

Dwayne's facial expression was similar to mine at the time he'd made his little announcement. It did not appear that he was tickled pink. His bodily gesture was not as secure as it had been inside of the airport terminal, or just five minutes ago when he dropped his bomb on me disguised as a surprise. I'd thrown him a curveball that he hadn't seen coming, not even with his perfect 20/20 vision.

"What the f-" Dwayne started, but then I cleared my throat, reminding him with my eyes that Kendra was present.

He'd been so worked up that he'd forgotten all about her even being there. He turned to look at Kendra, as did I. She still sat between us full of joy. She had no idea what I'd just said meant for our newly rejoined family. All she knew was that surprises were supposed to be a good thing.

Not wanting to spoil Daddy's little girl's mood, Dwayne forced himself to turn toward me. His smile was even more forced. I'm sure he had to muster up every ounce of strength he had to say to me, "Well, congratulations, baby, and good luck." And just to make sure Kendra didn't sense that anything was amiss, he leaned over and kissed me on the cheek.

This had to have been what the kiss of Judas felt like. I smiled inside.

"Thank you," I said as he pulled away. I looked at Kendra. "Now how about that banana split?"

"Yay!" she cheered.

I could feel Dwayne's eyes burning a hole through me as I got out of the car. Once he saw the conversation was over, he got out of the car and opened the door for Kendra. I was so glad that the discussion had been tabled, at least for now. But I knew come this evening when Dwayne and I were alone, things were going to get heated.

Chapter 7

Dwayne and Kendra settled in fine. The adjustment was not as stressful as I'd anticipated. Kendra made friends in the neighborhood. The hospital had a childcare facility for its employees, so Kendra spent some days there. Other times Tracy, being a part-time employee, had time to help out with Kendra, as did her sister that lived with her.

Dwayne was finishing up his two-weeks of orientation at the hospital. He was either putting on a front, or deep down inside he truly was trying to stay on my good side in an attempt for us to live happily ever after. Or maybe this was all the calm before the storm, because to my surprise, after we got home from the Dairy Queen the day they arrived in town, he never brought up the fact about me considering going to work for the hospital in Cleveland but once. And even then when he brought it up he wasn't tripping.

"We'll just cross that bridge when we get to it," was all he said, and then gave me that same kiss of Judas as he had before.

I'm telling you, it was a little scary; him being so understanding. Needless to say, for the past couple weeks I'd slept with one eye open. Even at work I made sure I didn't sleep on the ole Mister.

Although we were both assigned to the same department, Dwayne's orientation process prevented us from even seeing one another that much. Other than the lunchbreaks we shared together in the hospital cafeteria, we didn't see each other again until we got home. We drove separate only because there was no telling what type of emergency situation could pop up that could have either one of us at the hospital all night long.

So even though things seemed to be running pretty smoothly on the job, the upcoming week would be the test. Dwayne and I would be working together again like old times. We'd see each other more than on lunchbreaks.

"I enjoy our little lunches together," I found myself telling Dwayne just yesterday as we sat across from one another in the cafeteria. "It kind of feels like we're dating." I surprised my own self with the words I'd spoken. And from the expression on Dwayne's face, I'd surprised him too.

I figured that maybe seeing Dwayne more periodically throughout the day wouldn't be so bad. Kendra had been at her happiest having her mom and dad under the same roof . . . without incident. What she loved even more was settling into becoming a U.S. citizen, and that included trips to Walmart. A trip to Wally World was equivalent to a trip to Disney World in Kendra's eyes, and Dwayne didn't mind appeasing her. As a matter of fact, that's exactly where they were now. And everyone knows there is no in and out of Walmart. There was the issue of finding parking, the issue of going into the store to get one thing while getting distracted and buying a million other things, sometimes even forgetting what you went into the store to buy in the first place. The lines were never short and sweet, not even the self-check-out lines. Then of course there was the matter of finding your fricken car once you finished shopping. I figured they'd be gone two or three hours max. And I decided to take advantage of every minute.

I packed my overnight bag for tomorrow's trip to

Cleveland. Yes, the time had finally arrived for me to move toward that "bridge," as Dwayne had called it. It took all of fifteen minutes to pack since I was only planning to be there one night, then turn around and fly right back to Virginia the next day.

After I was all packed, I took a relaxing bath accompanied with music and wine. I figured I'd settle for something lighter than my usual Cîroc. I then tucked myself into bed, enjoying an empty home. I prepared my mind for sweet dreams, not the restless nights I'd experienced prior to Dwayne arriving. I was beyond blessed to have my daughter back with me. Believe it or not, Dwayne hadn't been that bad either, but my alone time was priceless. It allowed me just the rest I needed to get my mind right, as I had to get up at the crack of dawn to catch my flight to Cleveland. Between the effects of the wine and complete exhaustion due to closing up any loose ends at work, I was in a deep sleep within seconds of my head hitting the pillow.

When I woke up early that next morning to the sound of my alarm going off, I looked to see Dwayne snoring next to me. I hadn't heard nor felt him come in last night. That spoke volumes as to how worn out I was. But I was definitely refreshed now. I quietly climbed out of bed, put on my slippers, and headed to the restroom without Dwayne waking up. However, when I returned to get dressed, his spot on the bed was vacant.

"Dwayne?" I called out. I swept the room with my eyes only to find that he was no longer in the room.

I walked over to our bedroom door that had initially been closed, but was now cracked open. Upon sticking my head out of the door and into the hallway, I immediately smelled the aroma of bacon wafting through the air and delighting my nostrils.

I bit down on my bottom lip as I tried to contain my pleasure. Yes, I loved bacon, and my stomach definitely could have used a little somethin'-somethin' to settle the nerves that were trying to take over. But what really had me feeling all giddy inside was the fact that Dwayne was up and preparing breakfast for us. And I hadn't even given him any last night. With the way things were starting off this beautiful Friday morning, I couldn't say he'd have the same unlucky fate this morning as he did last night.

I continued to get myself ready. My flight was due to leave Norfolk Airport in three hours. I wanted to be at the airport at least an hour before my flight was scheduled to board. We were going to beat any heavy rush hour traffic by a couple hours, so I wasn't worried about that.

"Knock, knock," I heard Dwayne say as he entered the room with a tray in hand.

"Good morning, Chef Boyardee." I smiled, and then plopped down on the bed next to my overnight carryon bag as I stuffed my toiletry bag inside of it.

"Breakfast is served," he announced, "with all your favorites. Bacon, eggs, home-style fries, toast with light butter and jelly, and a glass of OJ that has a chill from sitting in the freezer for a minimum of thirty minutes."

I laughed as Dwayne walked over to me. "You are too much."

"And that's better than not being enough."

I could sense that he was getting a little serious.

"And I never want to be that guy for you who's not enough, Denise."

I looked downward so that he couldn't see me blush. The sincerity in his voice had me feeling some kind of way. I was salivating at the mouth over the delicious meal he'd presented me with, but I was getting moist in other places for other reasons.

"You've always been enough," I said, and I was telling the truth. Dwayne was a great guy. He was financially set, he wasn't abusive, he didn't do drugs, and he wasn't an alcoholic. He wasn't a cheater either, as far as I knew. He was a great provider and great father. I just think that when it came to me and Dwayne, somehow our romantic union turned into a business acquisition. We lost the fire. We lost the steam. With both of us having a military background, neither one of us knew how to turn it off in the home. Routine and strict structure carried over into our marriage. We gave orders and we took orders as if we were one another's subordinates and not husband and wife. And that's when the war in our home began.

It was a silent war. It was a power struggle that neither one of us were willing to lose. Unfortunately, our happily ever after was a casualty of the war, but it looked as though Dwayne was pulling out all the stops in order to resurrect it.

"Let's not even go there right now," Dwayne said as he set the tray on the bed, moved my bag onto the floor, and then placed the tray next to me. "I just want you to enjoy your breakfast. You've got a long day ahead of you, and you need to kick butt on this interview like I know you can."

I was surprised that Dwayne was still so encouraging when it came to my interview. I was for certain that deep down inside he was praying that I wouldn't get the job; and maybe he was. He was doing a damn good job of hiding it if that was the case.

"Here, now eat." He lifted a forkful of eggs to my mouth.

I looked down at the eggs smothered in cheese and onion. I then looked up at him. When I say every episode from those crazy ID Channel shows began to fill my head, I was not exaggerating. Instead of getting a divorce, was Dwayne trying to kill me? Had he weaseled his way back into my life so he could get close to me and do the deed? We did still hold pretty nice size life insurance policies on one another. Maybe that's why he couldn't have cared less that I was thinking about relocating to Cleveland. I'd be dead before the three men and a truck could even arrive with my belongings for me to get settled in.

I looked at the eggs again. I might not even make it off the flight to do the damn interview.

"What's wrong?" Dwayne asked. He looked down at the eggs. "Oh, shoot. My bad." He placed the forkful of eggs back on the plate while shaking his head. "You busted me."

My eyes nearly bucked out of my head. I couldn't believe Dwayne was about to admit to my suspicions.

"There goes my attempt to sabotage your interview." He looked up at me with an ornery look on his face. "I guess giving you onion breath right before your job interview was too obvious, huh?" He laughed. "The person interviewing you would have been too assaulted by your breath to even pay attention to your interviewing skills."

I feigned laughter as I watched Dwayne chuckle like Jolly old Saint Nick. I was relieved inside. I honestly thought this man was trying to kill me by poison.

"Here. Try the toast instead." He lifted the piece of toast to my mouth.

I sunk my teeth into the toasted delight. He'd made it exactly how I liked it. It was lightly toasted with a thin spread of butter and a dollop of grape jelly, spread evenly to each corner. My eyes rolled into the back of my head as I relished in something so simple, yet something I hadn't taken the time to make for myself since forever. It goes to show how we can often take the smallest things in life for granted.

"It is just how I like it," I said to Dwayne, a tad more

seductively than I meant to. I took a sip of my orange juice.

Dwayne licked his lips. "It's good to know that I haven't lost my touch."

"At least in that area, anyway." I was on a roll now. I couldn't keep the grown and sexy side of me at bay.

"Oh, we can definitely test out any other areas if you'd like to." Dwayne gave me the onceover with his eyes. "Well, would you like to?"

As I stared at Dwayne's thick lips and imagined them slurping my womanhood the way I'd slurped the orange juice out of the glass, I began to tingle. I never did understand how on some of those reality shows the couple could be estranged, fussing and fighting, calling each other out of their names, or just having problems in general one minute, but sexing up one another the next. I understood fully now.

In that moment, any negative or doubtful feelings I'd been having about Dwayne were out the window. All I could think about was him sexing me into a stupid stupor; sending me off on the flight of my life, both literally and figuratively.

I didn't even have to reply verbally. I think the look in my eyes spoke volumes as Dwayne stood, moved the tray of food from the bed to the floor, and assumed the position.

On his knees beside the bed next to the tray of food, Dwayne slowly spread my legs apart. I almost wished I'd worn something sexier than my Tweety Bird nightgown and my granny panties. I typically didn't even sleep in underwear. I'd purposely slipped into something less appealing, not wanting to tempt Dwayne into trying to get some. Now look who my little deed was backfiring on.

When it came to sex, I loved feeling sexy. After all, how can you engage in sex without the sexy? It went hand in hand if you asked me. The sexier I felt, the more of a show I could put on. I'm not sure how nasty I could get with the words, "I thought I taw a puddy tat," frolicking through my head. Then again, if I imagined Dwayne saying those words, it would be right on point, as he slipped my panties to the side and dove right into my puddy tat with his tongue.

"Ummm." I immediately moaned the moment the warmth and wetness of his tongue met the warmth and wetness of my clit. I cocked my legs open wider as I looked down and watched Dwayne go to work. "Yes, baby." And just like that, he was my baby again.

I began rocking my hips on the bed. I was rolling my hips like I was a Jamaican dance queen doing the dutty wind. I didn't have time to play around with it this morning. I had a plane to catch and I wanted to make sure I got mine in good before it was time to go. I grabbed Dwayne by his head and guided him up and down, up and then down again, making sure my hips rolled in sync with his head action.

"Mmm, you taste good," he said in-between licks and sucks. "I missed tasting you."

I needed him to shut up and eat up before he fucked my cum up. I liked to do all the talking while he was giving me oral sex. I needed him to put his mouth to other uses.

While having intercourse, he could talk as much smack as he wanted. As a matter of fact, I loved when he talked dirty, as long as I had already gotten mine in. Sensual verbal wordplay made him cum faster, sometimes too fast. I'd be right on the verge of my own climax and then there he'd go shooting off, getting all limp and stopping. I didn't care how quickly he popped off, as long as I had already been satisfied. I hated to say it, but nine times out of ten, when it came to Dwayne making me cum, it rarely happened through penetration. I usually had to wait until his ass went into the bathroom to clean up and then get my own self off real quick.

So since I hadn't gotten mine yet, I really needed him to

stay focused on the puddy tat.

"Shhh," I said softly. "Don't talk with your mouth full."

He snickered, but went to work with that magic tongue and those sucking skills.

"Ohhh. Ahhh." I moaned as my hips and his head line danced in perfect synchronization. "Yes, do that shit." I watched Dwayne's tongue Fa La La La La on my clit like he was auditioning for the New York Chamber Choir. I loved watching, but I couldn't help it any longer as I lost the strength in my neck and my head fell backward. "Oh, God. Yes. Oh, Dwayne. Oh Dwayne." The more I moaned, the faster he went until my throbbing clit exploded its sweet juices, wetness everywhere.

"Oh, fuck," Dwayne said, jumping up from between my legs and pulling his manhood through the boxers he was wearing. "I gotta swim in that pool right there. You're so fucking wet. Goddamn!" Dwayne was staring at my pussy while licking his lips as he stroked his stiffness.

Dwayne pushed me back on the bed and entered me in a single plunge. There was no sticking the tip in and playing around with it. All eight inches slid into my darkness like a contractor who had studied the blueprint and knew exactly where to go without directions.

"I missed the pussy," he said as he bucked in and out of me. "I missed my wife."

I wrapped my arms around his back and my legs around his waist as I enjoyed the sensation of his pelvis pressing against me and his vessel sliding in and out of me. I'd already cum, so now I could simply lay back and enjoy what felt good to me.

"Is it still mine?" Dwayne asked as he thrusted faster and faster, harder and harder. "Is it still mine?"

My head was lightly banging against the headboard as I

felt my titties jiggling through the gown. He was hitting it out of the ballpark.

"It's yours," I said. "Baby, it's yours." I might as well have been speaking in unknown tongues, because I didn't understand nor did I know what I was saying. I really needed someone to translate what the hell was happening here. While Dwayne was lost deep inside of me, I lost my fucking mind. That's what happens when a sistah gets some good dick. And, Lord have mercy, had I forgotten just how good Dwayne's dick was. Dick alone should have kept me with his ass.

"Oh shit, I'm cumming. I'm cumming," Dwayne roared as he did one final thrust and then remained stiff and hard inside of me as he released.

I tightened my legs around him with all the strength I had, pressing my throbbing clit against him so that I might receive some final pleasure from our intimate act. Seconds later, spent, the two of us lie in the bed, staring up at the ceiling, breathing heavily.

Once I'd come down off my climax and was in my right mind, I couldn't help but ask myself over and over, *What the fuck just happened?*

"You better get up and get moving," Dwayne said, rising up off the bed. "I'ma get cleaned up and then get Kendra up." He went into the bathroom, leaving the door cracked.

I sat up in the bed and my eyes caught him standing over the toilet releasing himself. All I could see was the back of him, his tight, brown ass cheeks with muscular dents in the sides of them. With all that pumping he'd just done, I could see how his muscles had formed. That's when a dark thought entered my mind. Since he hadn't been working those ass muscles out on me, who had he been working them out on? Now that I thought about it, for a man who hadn't had sex with his wife in as long a time as him, Dwayne had gone a good distance without busting a nut. Key words, though, "with his wife."

Just because Dwayne hadn't been sleeping with me didn't mean he hadn't been getting any. After all, that was pretty much the case when it came to me. I'd been living the single life since separating, in my mind and actions anyway. All this even though I had a marriage certificate that proved otherwise. Could I even think about getting upset with Dwayne for doing the same?

I snapped out of my thoughts when Dwayne flushed the toilet and walked over to the sink and turned on the water. I got out of the bed and made my way into the bathroom next while Dwayne went to go wake Kendra up.

Unlike Dwayne, who had been able to only take a bird bath, I had to hop in the shower and get cleaned up. A ho bath would not suffice considering I was about to travel by plane to another state. Neither did I want to feel icky between my legs, nor did I want the smell of sex exuding from my body. That would not have been fair to the passengers seated in my vicinity.

After I showered, we were all off to the airport. There was construction on the way, but it wasn't too bad. It only delayed us a few minutes to the point where once Dwayne pulled up to ticketing, I didn't have to rush.

"Have a safe flight," Dwayne said, handing me my luggage he'd retrieved from the backseat after opening the car door for me. He was such a gentleman. Breakfast in bed, good loving and chivalry. Why was I thinking about divorcing this man again?

"Yes, have a safe trip, Mommy," Kendra said.

"I will, sweetheart. I love you."

"Love you too."

Dwayne closed the passenger door. "Call me and let me

know when you've landed."

"I will."

This was the first sincere and awkward free conversation Dwayne and I had shared since his arrival in Virginia. Even lying in bed together had been awkward. But now things felt, well, they felt like old times; the old times as in back when we first met.

Dwayne was very kind and handsome back then. He still was. He was a southern man from North Carolina. He and his younger sister came from a family of successful professionals. Their mother was the former mayor of High Point, North Carolina and their father was a well- known, big shot criminal attorney. I admired his parents' thirty-five years of marital bliss. I would often observe the interactions of the two while visiting with Dwayne's family. Dwayne was such a creature of habit, just like his father. This part of him made for a very boring relationship. Everything had to be planned; no spontaneity whatsoever.

I smiled and then Dwayne kissed me on the lips as I headed into the airport. Through the glass automatic doors, I could see Dwayne standing there watching me walk away. He looked so sexy and so caring; like a husband should look when his wife is about to head off. It made me want to turn around, get back in that car, drop Kendra off at a babysitters or something, and then go home and do a repeat of our morning sexcapade. Maybe not even make it home, but pull over somewhere on the side of the road and have him top me off in the car.

Instead, I ordered my kitty to stop purring and went and checked into my flight. Once boarded and on the plane in my window seat, I couldn't shake thoughts of Dwayne. Even though he had me feeling on cloud nine right about now, I still could not eliminate the residue of uncertainty that was in my being.

In my heart, even now that I was sharing a bed with Dwayne, I couldn't help but wonder when all was said and done—when the effects of my orgasm were no more—would I go back to feeling as if he was nothing more than a business partner. Sure we'd probably have a dinner date or two. And if I had a say in the matter, we'd definitely have more sexual encounters, at least weekly. I wouldn't mind getting done right every day, but I didn't want to get tired of it either. I needed time to miss the dick to appreciate the dick. Then of course there would be the monthly shared household expenses. But all of that was so mechanical and routine.

Maybe we could switch it up a little bit and add a personal touch by me initiating the sharing of daily stories about patients and interactions at the hospital. Who was I kidding? Just like before, once the sex got old, so would our relationship. Then once again, whether Dwayne was lying next to me in bed at night or not, I'd find myself swallowed up by a feeling of loneliness.

As the plane headed down the runway, I began to accept loneliness as a fact of life. For now I'd make the most of the company I was keeping and enjoy it while it lasted.

Chapter 8

My flight landed fifteen minutes earlier than it had been scheduled to. That was a relief. I was already cutting it short when I planned to check into the hotel prior to going to the hospital for my interview. I knew there was a chance that my room might not be ready, but I was going to at least check my luggage in. It would have been far too unprofessional to show up for my interview looking like a bag lady with my luggage in tow.

Just as I had anticipated, my room wasn't available yet. It was still being cleaned by housekeeping. I was permitted to store my bags at the front desk though. Good thing, because now all I had to carry with me was my purse and small briefcase.

That extra fifteen minutes allowed me a tad bit more breathing room to taxi from the hotel to the hospital, and thank God too. There was a traffic jam at the exit ramp we had to get off of in order to get to the hospital. It set me back—you guessed it—fifteen minutes, which kept me right on schedule. Construction work or traffic jams couldn't stop this chick; not today. I had to laugh to myself thinking that if I got hired, this would probably be one of the only occasions I showed up on time, in spite of all the impediments.

I was able to enter the hospital and make my way to the

designated area as instructed by my POC without having to make up an excuse for being late. Now of course, being late would be something the staff at this hospital would have to get used to with me, just like back at Sentara, but that was something I'd rather they learn about me later than sooner. Didn't want anything jeopardizing my chances of getting the job. I'd prove to them that I was an excellent and hard worker. Like women typically do with their first love, I'd get them to adore me before showing them some of my bad habits that they'd eventually overlook.

"I'm here to meet with Dr. Thomas, the Medical Director of Pediatrics," I said to the receptionist behind the desk, giving her the name my POC had given me.

"Do you have an appointment?" she asked. She turned her attention away from me and then proceeded to tap on her computer keys as if I wasn't there.

"Actually, I have an interview with him." I smiled.

My statement perked her up somewhat. "Oh, okay." She looked from her computer screen to me, smiling and showing all thirty-one teeth. There was a gap so big that I was sure one tooth was missing; hence the thirty-one teeth showing instead of thirty-two. She quickly looked at the screen and then back at me. "Dr. Simpson?"

"Yes," I said proudly, all the while thinking, *Yeah, bitch, you better switch that attitude up. This time next month you could be working under me.*

"I'll let him know you're here." She stood. "Please have a seat." She extended her hand toward the waiting area. "And might I offer you coffee or something?"

Wow, before I was practically invisible, and now this chick was aiming to please. Humph. My reputation must have preceded me.

"No thank you," I said, "but I appreciate the offer." I

found a seat on one of the paisley upholstered chairs and then sat patiently while she went back over to her desk to inform Dr. Thomas of my arrival.

"He'll be right out," she said a few seconds later.

No sooner than I'd replied with the words "Thank you," Dr. Thomas appeared before me.

"Dr. Denise Simpson?" he greeted.

"Yes." I stood, looking him straight in his blueish-green eyes, mindful to keep great eye contact with him. I then shook his hand enthusiastically.

"I'm Dr. Thomas. What a pleasure it is to meet you."

"The pleasure is all mine, Dr. Thomas. Thank you so much for taking the time to talk with me about the position of Staff OB/GYN here at Rainbow Hospital."

"Thank you for coming."

I pulled my hand away from his that I thought he'd still be shaking now if I hadn't. He was matching my eye contact. I'm talking this guy would have definitely given me a run for my money back during the days of childhood staring contests. I didn't know if he was trying to intimidate me because I was an African American woman and he was the typical head white man in charge, but I was not backing down.

"Can I offer you coffee or anything?" He finally broke the stare first when he nodded and looked over his shoulder.

Black boss chick; one point. Head white man in charge; zip!

"Oh, no, I'm fine. Your receptionist already offered," I said.

He clasped his hands together. "Then I guess we can go ahead and get started."

"Absolutely," I agreed.

"Right this way." He led me to the frosted, closed door he'd come from behind. He opened the door, allowed me through first, and then said to the receptionist, "Katherine, be sure to hold all my calls, would you?"

"Yes, Sir," she said.

I waited by the door and allowed him to walk in front of me. Had he been a Black man, I probably would have walked in front of him, wiggling my ass in hopes of getting an advantage over the other candidates. But this guy looked like he didn't even eat chocolate-vanilla swirl ice cream cones, better yet get his sexual swirl on. I'd save my ass wiggling for when it could actually do me some good.

"My office is right this way," he said.

As he walked in front of me, he held light conversation as we made our way to his office. "Thank you, again, for taking time to come to Ohio. You live in Virginia, right?"

"I do."

"So it wasn't too bad of a flight, then."

"Just a little over three hours."

He stopped in his tracks once we arrived at his office door. "Good." He spun around and then said firmly, "So no using being jetlagged as an excuse if you bomb this interview."

I swallowed hard, a little taken aback by his comment and shift in demeanor.

"Just kidding." He let out a chuckle. "Come on in." He waved his hand for me to follow behind him as he entered his office.

I exhaled so loudly, I'm surprised I didn't blow him over.

"You know us doctors have to have a sense of humor." He sat in his desk chair. "Breaks up the monotony of some of the things we see throughout the day."

"I agree." Even though there were two chairs opposite side of the desk from where he was sitting, I remained standing. I'd learned job interview etiquette years ago and knew that the interviewee should remain standing until offered a seat. Job interview etiquette was also the reason why I'd turned down both Dr. Thomas's and his receptionist's offer of a drink. No matter how parched a person is or how addicted to caffeine they may be, decline all offers of food and beverage unless it's a lunch interview or something of that nature. Even if the interviewer is guzzling down a beverage or snacking on some vittles, decline, decline, decline!

"Please, have a seat." He extended his hand to the chairs I stood by.

"Thank you." I sat.

"I'm sure you've done your research, but let me tell you a little bit about Rainbow Hospital. In 2014, Rainbow was awarded Magnet status for Nursing Excellence." That was the nursing profession's highest national recognition by the American Nursing Credentialing Center, an arm of the American Nurses Association. Rainbow received re-certification in 2008 and 2014. The Hospital is also accredited by the Joint Commission on Health Care Organizations in addition to being ranked number two in *U.S. News & World Report's* 2014-15 Honor Roll of the nation's Best Children's Hospitals. We are very proud of our accomplishments, needless to say."

As I listened to Dr. Thomas, I watched him; his facial expressions and his movements. Even though he was of the opposite race, he reminded me so much of my husband in many ways, especially his mannerisms. I found myself picturing Dwayne sitting there instead of Dr. Thomas. Had my husband put it on me so bad that he had me seeing things? Seeing him!?

All of a sudden, as I observed Dr. Thomas, I felt an attraction forming. I promise on everything just seconds ago I'd been listening to this man with the utmost intensity, but now all I saw was his thin lips moving, and then imagining them doing a repeat of what Dwayne's had done to me that morning. From that thought I could not help but imagine what he held between his legs and what it would feel like between mine. I'd never been with a white man before, so I had no idea of how well or not so well they hung, but I was willing to find out firsthand.

Damn it, why couldn't I keep my lust demon under control? Now it was becoming more and more clear why Tracy said that I needed psychological counseling for my sexual appetite. First it was Dr. Cannon and now Dr. Thomas. And believe me when I say it wasn't just men in white coats that did this to me. It was any man that I thought might be able to allow me to reach the ultimate sexual pleasure.

I tried to maintain my composure and look like the professional woman that I was, or at least tried to be when I'd initially arrived for my interview. I was holding up pretty well on the outside as I sat there wearing my Neiman Marcus skirt suit. I was dressed to kill. And sure, maybe I had deliberately worn a skirt cut a tad higher above the knee than interview etiquette suggested. That was just in case Dr. Thomas had done his homework and someone back at Sentara had ratted me out about my habitual tardiness. If that was the case, I might have to use my feminine persuasion to land this job. It had been a minute since I'd had to stoop to such low tactics, but I knew all too well how to work this technique. It is what helped me get through undergraduate and graduate studies. I have no shame in my game, and as the old saying goes, sometimes a woman has to do what a woman has to do.

"Can I be honest with you, Dr. Simpson?" Dr. Thomas leaned in and asked.

Not sure where things were about to go, I figured now might be a good time to start turning on the charm. Figure I'd test my skills at getting him to come over to the dark side, if you know what I mean.

I slightly leaned in toward Dr. Thomas, and with a hint of seduction in my voice—where it could barely be detected—I said, "I would love for you to be honest with me, Doctor." I deliberately left off his last name so that it could be partially informal. Not disrespectful, just informal.

"I like you, *Doctor.*"

Touché.

"I like you too."

"From what I've seen"— He opened a folder that sat on his desk—"I think you'd be a perfect fit for Rainbow." He scanned the first page of the folder's contents and then looked back up at me. It was safe to say that must have been the folder that contained information about me and my work history. "I think you'd be a perfect fit for me. To work underneath me that is. I mean . . ." he cleared his throat, "with me."

Hmmm. Looks like all this chocolate was making Dr. Thomas a little nervous. Wasn't it the interviewee that was supposed to be nervous?

Black boss chick; two points. Head white man in charge; still zip!

I sat back comfortably in the chair. I was feeling confident now. I swear on everything had I been going commando, I would have pulled a Sharon Stone *Basic Instinct* on his ass. Instead, I left my legs crossed as they were and simply shifted in my seat.

"I think you'd be a perfect fit as well. I mean, I'd be a perfect fit." That was an honest mistake. I did not want to put it on too thick.

"If it were solely up to me, I'd be handing you a hospital badge right now."

I got excited. He sounded enthusiastic; like I was a shoe

in.

"But it's not up to me. I'm sorry to say, Dr. Simpson, but I can't offer you this job right now."

Chapter 9

M y insides deflated. I hid my true feelings under my game face and I continued listening.

"Before any final decisions are made," Dr. Thomas continued, "I'm required to introduce you to and have you interviewed by two other department heads."

I exhaled as best I could through my nostrils. Had I let the sigh of relief out of my mouth that I wanted to, poor Dr. Thomas would have thought he was caught up in a tornado. "It would be my pleasure," I lied. I was not in the mood to have to turn on the charm for two other folks.

Ten minutes later, a Dr. Charles Freeman and Dr. Ralph McClain joined in on the interview. Women had come very far in the medical industry, but clearly when it came to doctors, it was a male dominated field.

"So, Miss Simpson," Dr. Freeman started before Dr. Thomas immediately jumped in and interrupted.

"It's Dr. Simpson."

Dr. Freeman cleared his throat, having stood corrected. "Oh, my apologies, Dr. Simpson. No disrespect intended."

"None taken, Dr. Freeman," I replied, maintaining a level of respect for him even though I could tell the blond haired good ole boy didn't have much respect for women in general, let alone a Black woman.

Dr. Freeman continued. "Have you had any malpractice

suits filed against you?" He sat stoically waiting on my response.

"No, I have not," I answered. "No complaints to the board, nothing that has negatively affected my record." I figured I'd save him the time of asking so that he didn't have to go on a fishing expedition. I jumped right on the hook. No need to waste time.

"Describe what you liked about your first position as a doctor?" Dr. McClain took over.

From there both Dr. McClain and Dr. Freeman tag teamed me, firing off question after question.

"Tell us your least favorite job you have held?"

"Why are you deciding to leave your current position?"

I was firing answers right back at them just as quickly as they would shoot them off. As soon as one was asked, my answer followed. I was doing okay judging by the facial expressions and body gestures I received.

Although he never asked a single question, I could feel Dr. Thomas burning a hole through me with his eyes. If I didn't know any better, he was getting a hard-on watching me handle his colleagues how Li'l Kim used to claim in her rap lyrics she handled dicks.

The interview with the three doctors lasted about forty-five minutes, after which Dr. Freeman suggested I be taken on a tour of the hospital. When Dr. McClain didn't object, Dr. Thomas finally spoke.

"That sounds like a wonderful idea." Dr. Thomas stood and we all followed suit.

This was a good sign in my opinion. Why would they waste time taking me on a tour of the hospital if they'd already made their minds up that I wasn't the best candidate for the job?

We toured the hospital facility, which took up another

hour. To my delight, Dr. Freeman was only present the first half of the tour, then Dr. McClain was paged for an emergency shortly thereafter. Ultimately it looked as though this interview was ending the same way it had gotten started; with just me and Dr. Thomas.

"So what do you think, Dr. Simpson?" Dr. Thomas asked as he led me back to his office. "Could you see yourself joining the staff here at Rainbow?"

"Sure, as long as you all don't have some corny motto like 'Rainbow Hospital, where we treat you like the pot of gold.'"

We both started laughing. Interview Etiquette rule; only tell a joke if the interviewer has displayed that they have a sense of humor.

"You know, actually, that has a nice ring to it," he said. "I'm going to seriously think about submitting that to the board. It would look great underneath our logo." He stared off as if envisioning what it would look like.

I couldn't believe this man was serious. I'd only been joking, and now he was considering using my made up motto?

"What do you think?" he looked to me and said with a serious expression on his face.

"Well, I . . ." I was at a loss for words.

The corners of Dr. Thomas's lips raised into a smile. "Gotcha!" He pointed at me and burst out laughing.

I rolled my eyes up in my head and feigned being perturbed that he'd played a trick on me.

"Remember what we said earlier about having a sense of humor?" he reminded me.

"Yeah, yeah, yeah," I said, still acting as if I was upset.

We approached his office door.

"You're mad at me. I'm sorry." We both stepped into his office. "Why don't I make it up to you with lunch or something?"

I was shocked that he'd been so blatant in asking me out. The expression on my face mirrored my emotions.

"Not like on a date or anything," he cleared up. He went and sat down at his desk. I remained standing.

"Not like a date, huh? From the man who just participated in my being drilled about my entire life. You know practically everything there is to know about me. Why not take me out on a date at this point?"

"Not true. I mean, sure I learned a lot about you professionally, but there is plenty I could learn about you personally."

I was intrigued. "Oh yeah, like what?"

That's when the interview got personal.

Dr. Thomas began to ask me multiple questions in a quite inquisitive and authoritative tone. "Where are you from?"

"I'm from Pennsylvania," I said. "But I'm sure that's somewhere in that professional file of yours." I nodded down at the folder while holding eye contact.

"How many siblings do you have?"

"Two. A brother and a sister. The best of both worlds."

It was now feeling more like an interrogation, but in a fun way. So just as quickly as he was shooting his short, straight to the point questions at me, I was shooting him back the same kind of answers.

"What high school and college did you attend?"

Dr. Thomas was asking me questions that he had the answers to before I was ever even called in for an interview. And it didn't go unnoticed by me how of the million and one questions he'd asked me, not one of them had been about me having a husband and daughter.

I pulled my neck back and gave him the side-eye. "Dr. Thomas, now something is telling me that you are just talking to be talking. Surely all of the answers to your questions are buried somewhere in that file of yours." This time I tapped the folder with my well-manicured nails. "Soooo, are you talking to be talking at this point? I'm sensing an ulterior motive here." I made sure I had a smile in my eyes when I spoke. I didn't want the poor man to think I was trying to get him caught up in some type of sexual harassment situation.

He leaned back in his chair, staring at me. I could see the indention on his cheeks from him rolling his tongue around the inside of his mouth as he thought. Once the words that he'd gathered in his thoughts reached his mouth, placing his elbows on his desk and leaning forward, he spoke. "Okay, you've busted me. You're right. I'm sure all the answers to the questions I'm asking you are in this file . . . or that I already know the answers. It's just that I really enjoy talking to you. I can't say I've ever met a woman quite as intriguing as you."

I don't care what Dr. Thomas's mouth said, I'm sure this had everything to do with his pecker being intrigued by what was between a Black woman's legs. I bet it was driving him crazy wondering if once he went black, would he ever go back.

"So this whole wanting to get to know some personal things about me was nothing more than a ploy to get me to stay in your office?" I asked

He shrugged and unabashedly replied, "Pretty much."

I couldn't help but to blush. "But you know I can't stay here forever, Dr. Thomas, that is not unless you hire me. But I know, I know. You have to hash it over with your colleagues."

"That is true," he admitted, then leaned back into a comfortable position. "I do have an appointment coming up. But perhaps we can pick up where we left off this evening."

I raised an eyebrow. "This evening?"

"Sure, dinner instead of lunch. You ever heard of a dinner meeting or dinner interview?"

Indeed I had. Remember that little tidbit I mentioned earlier about not eating during an interview unless it was a lunch or dinner interview? Who knew this would turn into such?

"Do you really feel as if this interview needs to carry over into dinner? Is that what it's going to take to impress you enough for you to convince Dr. Freeman and Dr. McClain that I'm the right person for the job?"

"You remembered both the other doctors' names. I'm already impressed," Dr. Thomas said. "That's more than I can say for the last couple candidates I interviewed."

Dr. Thomas could sit there and play all the games he wanted to. I had this position on lockdown. I could feel it. At this point, it was clear that he had an attraction toward me and wanted to abandon the entire professional side of my visit and move on to the personal. My only dilemma now was whether or not to play the game.

Initially my entire focus and goal was to come to Cleveland, kill this interview, resulting in a contract with the hospital. How was I supposed to know I was going to be attracted to the damn interviewer and want to play in the snow? Now I found myself living out that old cliché about being in between a rock and a hard place. I'd been flirting and playing coy with Dr. Thomas all this time. If I were to cut it off now, would that jeopardize me not being hired? I may have memorized all the etiquette rules of an interview, but what I failed to think about was once starting this little game, how in the world, and when, was I supposed to end it?

"I hope you don't find it rude, but I need to excuse myself so that I can go to the little girls' room." I needed a minute to think without him staring down my throat. Besides that, I really did have to pee. I stood. I was not asking permission. I needed to get out of there. I needed a moment to do something I should have done prior to sitting my ass down in his office; come up with a game plan, a full game plan, and execute it. Every business strategy required an exit strategy.

"Oh, by all means." He stood. "Do you remember where it is? Just right down the hall to the-"

He must have seen the wheels turning in my head trying to recall exactly where the bathroom was.

"I'll just show you." He walked around his desk and over to the door.

"Thank you. I appreciate it."

"No problem. It gives me a chance to ask you a few more questions." He stopped in his tracks. "Then again, that might not be too smart. We won't have anything to talk about in order to justify continuing our interview over dinner."

"You're right about that." I smiled, pointed for him to take the lead, and then proceeded to follow behind him up the hall.

"It's right here." When he stopped in front of the restroom, he placed his hand on the small of my back, as if guiding me. Who was he kidding? I knew he was trying to get a free feel. But there was no complaining on my part, nor did I try to move away from his touch. The only thing I did was melt a little bit inside at the feeling of his flesh being ever so gently pressed against me.

"Thank you." I smiled and then walked away toward the door. Even though his hand was no longer on my back, I could feel the impression of it.

The first thing I did once I entered the bathroom was make sure that no one else was in there. There were only two stalls and I saw no feet under either door. I immediately let a huge gust of wind escape my mouth. "Whew weee."

I needed to catch my breath and get my head right. What was I going to do with this man? There were so many pros and cons to my throwing caution in the wind and going out on a date with him. We were getting along great playing our little game of cat and mouse, but what if things went totally left, therefore ruining any chances of me getting the position at the hospital?

Then let's say we have a wonderful evening with a happy ending, because let's face it, neither one of us were going on this dinner date slash interview simply because we were hungry and wanted to talk. There was an attraction between us so strong that there was no way we were going to be able to end the evening without jumping each other's bones.

The same way we were going into this thing as mature adults, surely we could exit the same way. I hadn't looked down at his hand to see if he was wearing a wedding ring or not, so I don't know whether he had a wife and kids to go home to, but he sure as hell knew that I did. With that being said, I was probably stressing out for nothing. Not that I was bragging, but I had been with men outside of my marriage. The difference was that I never had to see them again, let alone work with them. It was clear I was not going to get anywhere going back and forth in my own head.

After taking care of my business, I washed my hands and glanced at myself in the mirror. "What's happening to me?" I asked my reflection in the mirror. What was wrong with me? I was a married woman for Christ's sakes; a married woman who had agreed to reconcile with my once estranged husband. Yet here I was hours away from having dinner with my perspective colleague. I searched my eyes trying to figure out what exactly I was in search of. I had to be looking for something. Was I looking for it in men when I needed to be looking within myself?

Growing up, I missed out on having a father figure in my life. Or at least I think I missed out. It's hard to miss something I never had. Yes, there were a handful of times I sat and thought about how different life might have been for me had my father not abandoned me. But wallowing in pity wasn't my thing. So I'd quickly brush off yesterday's woulda, coulda, shouldas and press forward.

I'm not sure if one would label me as a chick with "daddy issues," but I definitely had issues, and sooner rather than later, they were going to land me in big trouble.

Chapter 10

My thoughts were getting way too deep. Sounded like I was in need of a therapy session, but for now, Dr. Thomas was waiting. I exited the restroom.

"Oh, my. I'm sorry," I said when I walked out of the door and practically smacked right into Dr. Thomas. "I didn't expect you to still be out here waiting on me. What? Afraid I wouldn't find my way back to you?"

"Not at all," he said. "It's just that I brought you here, and no way did I intend on leaving you."

"Well, I hope I didn't make you wait too long." I feigned fixing my hair, patting the left side and then the right.

"You're worth the wait. And your hair looks fine."

He complimented me on my hairstyle, my perfectly arched eyebrows, and French manicure. "You are one well put together woman." He gave me the same onceover he'd given me before showering me with all those compliments. "Your husband is a lucky man."

And there he'd finally said it. He'd mentioned the elephant in the room, or should I say back in Virginia.

"So, uh, you never quite confirmed whether or not you were going to have dinner with me," he continued on. Good thing too, because I did not want to verbally acknowledge him mentioning Dwayne. "But I'll tell you what. While you were in the ladies' room, I made myself a reservation for tonight at the Blue Pointe Grille downtown."

I listened as he continued, even though I knew exactly where this was headed.

"We both know it's not a dinner interview. Like I said before, I know everything I need to know about you to know that you've got a 'yes' from me. But let me talk to my colleagues this afternoon, and if our discussion goes as well as I think it will, tonight's dinner will be more like a celebration."

"A celebration, huh?"

"Yes. A celebration of you getting the position here at Rainbow."

With his last statement, I kind of sensed that there would be some strings attached on how well his conversation would go with Dr. Freeman and Dr. McLain based on whether I'd be joining him for dinner. It was confirmation when he whispered in my ear, "So will I see you at dinner tonight to celebrate?"

"So you're that confident in how your discussion with the doctors is going to go?"

"I'm just as confident that the position is yours as you were when you walked into my office today."

I had to smile on that note. If he hadn't noticed anything else about me, I'm sure glad that my confidence in myself and my work stood out. "Then I guess I'll see you tonight."

Dr. Thomas walked me back to his office where I retrieved my briefcase. I then headed back out to the receptionist's desk where I asked her to call me a taxi.

As I stood in the hospital lobby staring out of the glass doors while waiting on my taxi, I immediately wanted to kick myself. I had agreed to have dinner at what sounded like a pretty decent restaurant, and here the only thing I'd packed was a Bebe jogging suit to wear back on the plane tomorrow.

Instantly my mind began racing. Here I was in Cleveland

with its unpredictable weather. I knew as much because I'd been tracking the city's weather in determining what I was going to wear to the interview. Now I had to figure out what to wear for dinner tonight. Not only that, but I'd have to come up with something to tell Dwayne as well. I was going to be MIA for a few hours this evening. And if Dwayne called me as much as he had right before his moving to Virginia, no way was I going to be able to explain my unaccounted for time.

I pulled out my cell phone to call Dwayne to get the conversation over with, but then thought better of it. I'd wait for him to call me, and when he did, I'd pour it on thick about how tired I was. How I was just getting out of the interview that involved me being drilled by three doctors and a full tour of the hospital. The cherry on top would be me saying how all I wanted to do was get back to the hotel and sleep until it was time to get up for my flight. Satisfied that he'd buy it, I went on to my next dilemma.

I pulled up the internet on my phone and looked up the nearest mall. That would be my first stop before heading back to the hotel. As luck would have it, there was a fricken mall attached to the hotel. A casino too. The basketball arena was even attached. The combo was called Tower City Center. I hadn't even realized that when booking the hotel. The Renaissance is one of my favorite hotel chains to stay at. I'm very familiar with their quality and amenities, so I didn't have to worry about researching what they did and did not offer. Besides, I was only going to be in town for one night, so it wasn't that serious. I had no idea I'd end up spending my one night on the town.

Knowing the hotel was attached to the mall, I went ahead and checked into my hotel room before going shopping. I went to my room and put on my sneakers. I was not about to go traipsing around that mall in my heels. I'd already done that touring the hospital, and my dogs were barking!

By four o'clock that afternoon, I was back at my room. It wasn't a full minute before I'd collapsed on the bed and was staring up at the ceiling before I could hear the buzzing of my cell phone. I snapped my head up and looked around. I sat up in the bed and listened to the buzzing sound. I looked down at my purse I'd dropped on the floor at the foot of the bed. I hurriedly dug into the purse to get my phone before it went to voicemail. Fearing I didn't have time to look at the caller ID before the call went to voicemail, I immediately answered it.

"Hello. This is Dr. Simpson." Not knowing who may have been calling me, I used my safe, professional greeting.

"Well, hello, Dr. Simpson. It's good to know that you are still alive and breathing here on planet earth."

"Dwayne," I said. "Hey." I cradled the phone between my ear and my shoulder, still holding it with one hand, as I began taking my shoes off my feet. "I was about to call you," I lied. Well, it wasn't a total lie. I was about to call him earlier from the hospital lobby, after my interview.

"About time, considering I've only called you a thousand times. Had me worried sick. I didn't know if your plane had landed, got stuck in the air, or what?" He had a joking tone, but I could tell he was somewhat serious and even a tad perturbed.

I pulled the phone away from my ear and checked my missed calls. Damn! Dwayne had called me six times. I had six text messages too. I could only assume those were from him as well. He'd probably sent me a text after each call. I placed the phone back to my ear.

"Sorry," I apologized. "I put my phone on vibrate when I went into the interview and I forgot to take it off. I haven't heard my phone ring." I thought for a second and then continued on with my plan. "Not that I would have been able to answer the phone anyway. Believe it or not, I'm just getting back to the hotel." I'm so evil, and proof of that was the wicked grin that spread across my lips as I allowed that lie by omission to fall off my lips. The truth was that, yes, I had just gotten back to my hotel room. The lie by omission was that I hadn't just gotten back from my interview, which I'm sure Dwayne assumed, and of which I was going to allow him to.

"Really? Wow, that's a mighty long interview."

"It was. After my interview with the initial hiring physician, I had to interview with two others. Then after that they took me on a tour of the entire hospital."

"Well, all of that only means one thing."

"What?" I began to rub my foot.

"You know what it means. Quit trying to be humble. That job is as good as yours. Nobody is going to spend their entire day with someone who they don't plan on hiring. Trust me, you wouldn't have even made it to the second set of interviews, let alone a tour of the facility if you weren't the number one candidate. You would have gotten an escort to the front door is about it." Dwayne laughed.

"Yeah, maybe you're right." Now I was deliberately playing humble. "We'll see."

There was silence.

"You know what it means if you get this job, don't you?" Dwayne asked and then continued without even allowing me to answer. "It means we'll be right back to where we were not too long ago. Married living estranged. That's something we really have to think about."

I held my silence. I was not trying to get into this right now. Apparently Dwayne was.

"I really feel like we are in a good place, better than we have been in a long time. Putting aside how I feel, I'm not sure how Kendra would react to this."

Okay, there he went bringing my baby up again. It was definitely time to end this conversation before guilt took over and kept me from a wonderful evening with Dr. Thomas. I'd already invested a hundred dollars at Macy's on a dress for tonight's dinner. And as hungry as I was, I'd decided not to grab something from the food court at the mall so that I wouldn't feel fat in the damn dress. So no way was I going to let Dwayne get into my head and keep me from a night of fun in Cleveland, Ohio.

"You're right, that really is something we have to think about." I yawned. "But not right now. I'm exhausted. I need to think about this with a clear head. All I want to do is climb in this bed and not get out of it until I have to get up in the morning to catch my flight."

"I understand." I could hear the disappointment in Dwayne's tone.

"It may be a conversation we might not even have to have. I have not even been offered the job yet."

Dwayne sighed. "I guess you're right. Maybe we should table this conversation."

"Maybe we should. But for now, I'm going to shower, grab me a bite to eat, get in this bed, and I'll call you in the morning." What? I did plan on doing all of the above . . . with a couple things in between and not necessarily alone.

"Okay. Do you want to speak with Kendra before you turn in?"

"Of course." I was actually about to ask him to put her on the phone.

"Hold on."

A few seconds later Kendra was on the phone telling me how much she missed me and couldn't wait for me to get back home. I dittoed her sentiments before ending the call. I spread my arms as if I was going to up and fly away, then

I crashed backward on to the bed. My conversation with Dwayne had exhausted me that much more. When the elders tell us that marriage is hard work, they aren't lying. But what's even harder is working on a broken marriage, which takes me back to another saying; some things can't be fixed. You've gotta know when a broken toy can't be fixed and needs to be thrown away. Maybe that's what my marriage was; the broken toy that couldn't be fixed. Or maybe deep inside it was me who didn't want it fixed so that I could keep playing with other toys.

Chapter 11

After getting off the phone with Dwayne I took a little cat nap. I set my alarm to wake me, because I knew if I hadn't, the lie I'd told to Dwayne would have turned into the truth. I wouldn't have made it out of that bed. I would have been in one of my alcohol induced comas without having partaken in the alcohol. The day had been just that long. But I wasn't an old lady turning into bed early this evening. All I needed was a second wind and then I'd be good to go.

When the alarm on my cell phone went off, you have no idea how bad I wanted to do my norm and hit that snooze button. The last thing I wanted to do was give sign that I had an issue with being prompt. As far as I knew, for Dr. Thomas, this really might have been an extension of our interview. So spite what my body was telling me to do, I obeyed my mind and hit the button to turn the alarm off and then got out of bed.

Ten minutes later, after exiting the shower, I was feeling renewed and refreshed as if I'd enjoyed a full eight hours of rest. I slipped on the new plum dress I'd purchased at the mall. I'd contemplated on a red one that fit me a little snug, which made me look as if I had curves for days. It would have been having Dr. Thomas offering me that job for sure, but it was a bit too pricey to be spending on a one night man.

I recalled Dr. Thomas telling me that Blue Point Grille,

where we were to meet for dinner, was downtown, but I wasn't sure where about downtown. Cleveland had a pretty nice size downtown area. Riding in from the airport, I couldn't help but to admire the beautiful skyline. I was about to get on my phone and Google the distance, but then decided to call the hotel front desk instead. Since they lived here, they'd be able to give me an idea.

"It's only a couple blocks up," the front desk told me. "In walking distance actually, but by all means we can arrange for a taxi to pick you up."

"Oh, no, that's okay," I said. "If it's as close as you say it is, I don't mind catching a little fresh air."

"Yes, Ma'am, but don't hesitate to let us know if you change your mind."

I ended the call and went to put on fresh makeup. After beating my face, I stared at myself in the mirror. I debated on whether I should do a little something different with my hair. I'd worn it in a bun during the interview, but if I took the bobby pins out, I'm sure my ends would have a little curl to them and lightly dust my shoulders.

"Too much," I said to my reflection, deciding to leave it as is. I hated the fact that I hadn't packed any extra jewelry. I think my diamond studs set in white gold would have gone better with the dress since all I had were the black pumps I'd worn during the interview. I had my sneakers, but that wouldn't have worked of course. The diamond studs set in yellow gold would have to do.

It was when I went to slip my shoes on that I had second thoughts about walking to the restaurant. Thoughts of how badly my feet had ached earlier thanks to these shoes came to mind. With that thought, I picked up the phone and asked the front desk to have a taxi waiting on me out front at 6:55. If I could walk to the restaurant in just a few minutes, then surely the taxi could get me there in at least two. I was cutting it close, but I simply couldn't shake this antipathy that was going on between me and time.

I gave myself a final onceover and then headed to the front lobby of the hotel. On the elevator ride down to the lobby, an emotion regarding Dwayne took over me that I hadn't experienced since our separation. Guilt. This wasn't the first time I would have been with another man other than Dwayne since we exchanged wedding vows. But it was the first time I'd felt guilty about it. And it was the first time where it actually felt like cheating.

"But you haven't even done anything yet," I told myself. "It's just dinner." I managed to shake off those crazy feelings as the elevator doors opened.

Once I made it to the front lobby door, I was so glad I'd decided to call a taxi. The month of March was no joke in Cleveland. We'd be going into April in a couple days, yet here in Cleveland it still felt like the dead of winter. Earlier I'd been deceived by the bright, beautiful sun shining, that and my distraction of plotting untruths in my head about my unofficial date to notice that it wasn't the warmest of months. Then again I'd had on my suit jacket and really hadn't been outside of a building or vehicle long enough to be bothered. But now, in this evening cold, not even the long sleeves on my dress could fight off the air from biting down into my flesh.

I thought about running back up to grab the wool poncho I'd brought, not with Cleveland's cold temperature in mind, but the coldness I usually suffered on the aircraft. Seeing that the taxi was right outside waiting and only a few feet away, I figured I could stand the cold for a mere few seconds. That and the fact I was getting curb service to the restaurant door. So I stepped out the hotel and did a powerwalk toward the taxi. When the driver saw me coming, he hurried out of the driver's seat to open the back passenger door for me.

"Thank you," I said, hopping straight into the back." Once I got snuggled inside and realized the car was nice and toasty, I made a mental note to tip this cabbie, even if he was only driving me a stone's throw away.

"Blue Point?" the driver confirmed once he was back behind the steering wheel.

"Yes." I nodded.

"I know it's close, but there is a minimum ten dollar charge." He pointed to a sign posted on the dash above the meter. "Not my rule. Company rule."

"That's no problem at all," I told him. "I completely understand." And I did. What cabbie could make a living being nickeled and dimed by driving folks back and forth up the block?

I swear I had just clicked my seatbelt when I heard the cab driver say, "Here you are, Ma'am."

Hell, maybe my ass could have walked. I dug in my purse for the ten dollars. I happened to look up at the fare to see that it wouldn't have even been five dollars had they not had that policy in place. So the battle began in my mind; to tip or not to tip. In my thinking, he was getting a five dollar tip, but at the end of the day, he had to report that ten dollar fare to his company, so actually he wasn't. So with that, I stuck to my initial mental commitment and threw in two extra bucks for the tip.

A sudden rush of cold air slapped the shit out of me as the driver opened the car door for me. I should have gone back for that damn poncho.

I hurriedly slid out of the car with money in hand, immediately handing it to the driver and speed walking to the restaurant door.

"Thank you, Ma'am," I heard the driver say from behind

me. "Here is your receipt. It's my card, too, just in case you need transportation elsewhere." He was writing on the card as he spoke.

I slowed and turned on my heels. The driver was walking toward me, and there was no way I was going to even go meet him halfway. I continued backpedaling slowly to the restaurant door, causing the driver to have to come farther and farther away from his car.

His hand extended the card and I reached out and scooped it up, quickly whipping around and opening the restaurant door. I wasn't completely rude, though. I did manage to throw a, "Thank you. I'll call if I need you," over my shoulder, and then placed the card in my purse.

Once inside the restaurant with the door closing behind me, separating me from the winter hulk on the other side, I shook off the chill, rubbing my arms like I was trying to start a fire. I looked down at my watch. It was six fifty-nine. Yay me! I still had a whole minute to spare. I was doing pretty damn well today if I didn't say so myself. I guess Father Time figured if I could patch things up with Dwayne, then he and I had a chance at reconciliation too.

I needed that minute to get warmed up so that I could stop feeling like a Popsicle.

"Welcome to Blue Point Grille."

I looked up to see a gentleman wearing a white shirt, black tie, and black slacks. He stood behind a clear podium that had the restaurant name and logo engraved on it.

"Do you have reservations?" he asked.

"No," was the first thing that came out of my mouth. "I mean, I don't, but the party I'm meeting, I believe, made reservations. His name is Dr. Thomas."

"Oh, yes. Dr. Thomas is already seated."

Damn it! Even when I was early I was late. Go figure. I

know it was only one minute, but for me that was like an hour.

"He's been waiting for your arrival." The gentleman smiled. "Come right this way please."

As I followed the restaurant host, I took in the décor and ambiance of the place. It was a lovely, elegant, multilevel restaurant. On the first level there was a live band playing smooth jazz in the dimly lit room. The stage had red and blue lights highlighting the silhouette of each band member.

The host led me to the upper level of the restaurant where the towering windows overlooked the city. Dr. Thomas was sitting in a booth. Once he saw me approaching, he stood. I noticed how he tried to keep eye contact with me, but his eyes couldn't help but travel the length of my body.

I cleared my throat to bring his eyes back up to mine.

"Oh, sorry," he apologized. "You look simply stunning."

"Thank you," I said as the host pulled my chair out for me and I took my seat.

"You're server for the evening will be Jennie, and Jennie will be right with you."

"Thank you, Kent," Dr. Thomas said to the host.

It didn't go unnoticed by me that Kent and Dr. Thomas seemed to have a rapport and degree of familiarity with one another.

"So you come here often?" I asked, settling comfortable into my chair.

"Only on special occasions," he said with a knowing look in his eyes.

"Ooooh, does that mean you consider me special?"

"But of course." Dr. Thomas had already taken his seat. He looked up as a girl dressed like Kent, only she was wearing a skirt instead of slacks, approached the table.

"Dr. Thomas, you're favorite." She shot Dr. Thomas a huge smile as she placed an empty wine glass in front of each of us. She immediately began to pour.

"Thank you, Jennie," Dr. Thomas said.

I couldn't tell if he was familiar with Jennie or if he knew her name because Kent had previously mentioned it, that and the fact that it was on her nametag.

I watched the clear wine fill each glass halfway.

"I hope you don't mind," Dr. Thomas said. He pointed to the wine. "But I took the liberty of ordering us a cocktail. Do you drink?"

"I don't mind at all," I said. "And I definitely enjoy a nice glass of wine." I would have preferred Cîroc of course, maybe apple flavored.

"Good." He looked relieved.

"I'll give you two a minute to go over the menu," Jennie said, "And then I'll be back to take your order." She looked from Dr. Thomas to me. "Can I start you off with any appetizers?"

Dr. Thomas looked to me.

"I'm fine," I said even though I was anything but. I was hungry, but I didn't want to go out like Miss Piggy.

Dr. Thomas looked up at Jennie. "No appetizers this evening. The wine will be fine for now."

"Wonderful," Jennie said. "I'll be back in a bit."

I took a sip of the wine as Jennie walked away. "Mmm. This is delicious."

"I'm glad you like it," Dr. Thomas said, after taking a sip from his own glass. "Not everybody enjoys dry wine."

"Yeah, well, I'm not necessarily the sweet kind of girl," I said, lifting the glass back to my lips. "When it comes to wine anyway."

"Are you teasing me, Dr. Simpson?" he leaned in and said with a raised eyebrow.

I mirrored his action. "Why no, Dr. Thomas."

He smirked then sat back. "We're no longer at the hospital, so you don't have to be so formal. Please, call me Bernard."

"Okay, Bernard." I took another sip of my wine.

"Aren't you going to return the gesture by allowing me to call you by your first name?"

I placed my glass on the table, savoring the wine that slid down my throat before speaking. As I swallowed, I simply shook my head. Once the wine had slithered down my throat I spoke. "Un umm. I like the way you say 'Dr. Simpson.'"

"I see. Very well then. Dr. Simpson it is."

Bernard took a sip of his wine, glancing at me over the rim of his glass.

I turned away as I blushed. I felt like a ninth grader standing at my locker when all of a sudden the senior star quarterback struts down the hallway and notices me.

"Why do you keep looking away?" he asked.

"Why do you keep staring at me?" I answered his question with a question of my own.

"You are so beautiful. You look good enough to eat." He was looking at me like I was a piece of meat. "I think you'd go better with this glass of wine than anything on the menu."

Bernard was coming on a little bit stronger than I was used to. But I liked it. He was so sharp and quick with it. He was definitely keeping me on my toes. I had to admit, though, that it was becoming harder and harder to form comebacks just as quickly. This must have been what it felt like to be in a rap battle.

As I looked at him, I noticed that even though he was facing me, he was staring over my shoulder. I know the hell he wasn't eyeballing some other chick right in front of my face. I immediately snapped my neck around to see what had pulled his attention from me.

"Oh my," I said as my eyes lit up. I couldn't blame him for

gazing at such a beautiful arrangement.

"For the lady?" the man approaching the table asked, looking at Bernard while nodding toward me.

Bernard smiled at the man and then nodded toward me as well. "Yes."

I gasped and placed my hand on my heart when the gentleman placed the vase of deep, ruby red roses on the table. They were sprayed with greenery and baby's breath. The roses were huge and fully open. They were so thick, as if a million petals were on each rose.

"These are absolutely beautiful," I said. My eyes sparkled. I could not take my eyes off of the beautiful bouquet. The aroma wafted through the air, seducing my nose. Seducing all my senses, which I'm sure was exactly what the good doctor had wanted to achieve with his act of kindness.

"I'm glad you like them," Bernard said as he pulled out his wallet and tipped the gentleman before he walked away.

"I love them. They have to be the most beautiful roses I've ever seen. It's like somebody sat and watched these things grow, caring for them every second without letting them out of their sight. They are simply perfect."

"Just like I've been telling you that you are."

I was able to tear my eyes away from the flowers and look at Bernard. "No, you said I was perfect for the job."

"And that's true, which is why I ordered you the flowers."

At first I squinted my eyes in confusion. I wasn't making the connection between me being perfect for the job and him giving me roses. Then it hit me. "Are these roses for what I think they are? Are they to congratulate me?" I waited on pins and needles as Bernard stared at me with a teasing look. "Well?"

"It is with pleasure, and with the support of both Dr. Freeman and Dr. McClain, that I offer you the position of

Staff OB/GYN at Rainbow hospital."

Yes! I screamed in my head, but then kept my composure enough to reply calmly. "And it is my pleasure to accept," I said, and then I realized that we hadn't even gone over any of the terms of my employment. "I mean, first I guess I need to know a few important details like-"

"It's a three year contract. Ten thousand above the listed pay for when you first applied. That was based on your work experience and references." Bernard rattled off a few other bits and pieces of information concerning the job. All but one really major one.

"When would you need me to start?" That right there could be the deal breaker. Before, I wouldn't have thought twice about it. I would have immediately accepted the positon, packed Kendra up, and we would have been on the first thing smoking to Cleveland. But it seemed as though I had some unforeseen extra baggage I'd acquired since applying for the job.

With Dwayne committed to work at Sentara and me agreeing to give our marriage another try, I had no idea how this was going to work out.

"Is everything okay?" Bernard asked.

I must have been subconsciously frowning.

"Is it the money? Is that an issue, because if it is-"

I put my hand up. "No, no. It's not the pay. The pay is great."

"Then what is it? Your excitement seemed to dissolve as if it was something I said."

"No, no. I'm just in shock is all. This is wonderful news." I picked up my glass of wine. "Why don't we toast?"

Bernard picked up the bottle of wine and topped off both our glasses.

"To the newest member of the Rainbow staff." He raised

his glass.

"To me," I said with a modest shrug, raising mine.

"To you."

We clinked our glasses and then drank. By now I was already feeling good from the buzz of the wine. I wasn't about to mess up the feeling thinking about Dwayne. Nobody told him to apply for a job in Virginia. That was on him. Right now I was having a celebration dinner for my official job offer right here in Cleveland, Ohio. And if all ended well, dessert would come in the form of an orgasm.

Chapter 12

Thank you so much, Dr. Thomas," I started and then corrected myself. "I mean Bernard. This really is great news."

"It is indeed." He winked.

Bernard was a smooth operator, literally, considering he was one of the head pediatric surgeons at the hospital. He'd not only arranged for dinner at this lovely restaurant, but he'd also arranged for a dozen long stem, red roses to be delivered to congratulate me on my new position. And did I forget to mention the delicious wine? He was playing all the right notes to my favorite tune.

I once again leaned in to take in the aroma of the bouquet.

"Are you two ready to order?"

I had honestly forgotten all about Jennie. I hadn't even bothered to look at the menu, so I ordered something I knew I couldn't go wrong with; steak. Bernard never even had to open the menu before rattling off his order to Jennie. He probably knew the thing by heart.

"I'm going to go put in your entrees," Jennie said. "Can I get you anything else for now?"

Bernard reached for the bottle of wine and held it up. There was probably a half glass left. He looked at me. "Maybe another bottle?" He was questioning me with his eyes.

"Oh, no, I'm fine." I lifted my glass that he'd just practically filled up. "This should get me through the night."

He shot me an ornery look. "But what if I was trying to get you through the morning?"

I smiled and shook my head at his mischievousness. "In that case, why not order another bottle?"

"I'll bring it right out," Jennie said, walking away from the table.

Having been totally oblivious to the fact that the restaurant was pretty full, I took a look around. Everyone seemed to be all smiles. There must have been a lot of celebrating going on in Cleveland tonight.

I turned my attention back to the table where the flowers beckoned for my attention. Just looking at the beauty of what nature could create put me on a high. I was way up on cloud nine. It must have been a woman thing, but there was something about receiving flowers. Food might be the way to a man's heart, but flowers were definitely a way to a woman's. Tonight they certainly made mine skip a beat.

"You don't get flowers often, huh?"

Bernard's inquiry pulled my attention away from the bouquet. "Why do you ask that?"

"Every time you look at them your eyes get almost as huge as the roses." He let out a chuckle.

I had not seen a dozen of roses meant for me since the day I gave birth to Kendra. Dwayne wasn't the flower giving kind of guy. Not even when he screwed up did he give me the typical "I'm sorry" bouquet. Then again, that was probably because Dwayne never really messed up.

Dinner at a nice restaurant, I totally expected from Bernard. He didn't seem like the person who went cheap. I could tell by the diamond watch he wore. I'd peeped that out during the interview. Even though he'd worn a white doctor's coat during our interview, I could tell it was custom made. His name was even stitched on the left pocket. No cheap badge would suffice in letting the world know who he was.

The flowers, though, had been totally unexpected. I felt special. Even though Dwayne had never done anything to piss me off or disrespect me during our marriage, he never made me feel special. I suppose what a man doesn't do is as equally important as what he does do.

Why was I thinking about the rollercoaster of a marriage Dwayne and I had been riding? I never realized until this moment that throughout the marriage I'd been so emotionally incomplete. Sexually too. Dwayne could lay the pipe. He was working with just enough inches. But after a while it became routine. There was no passion involved.

Deep down inside I must have been longing to be made to feel complete. Why else was I so willing to cheat on my husband with a stranger that had only given me flowers . . . not his heart?

"You know you didn't have to buy roses for me," I said, avoiding having to answer Bernard's question of whether I received flowers often or not. I figured it was his way of trying to point out the fact that he'd done something that my husband probably doesn't do.

"Oh but I did," he said. "And I have more where those came from."

"More flowers? Are we celebrating something else I don't know about?"

"No," he said frankly, then drank some of his wine.

"Then why more flowers?"

"A woman as beautiful, smart, hardworking, and as talented as you should receive flowers just because it's Tuesday. But it's not necessarily more flowers that I have for you. Just more."

Thank God Jennie showed up with the bottle of wine. Her approaching captured Bernard's attention and allowed me time to wipe the drool from my mouth. This man had me captivated. Sure he had to know that I was leaned more toward giving him a bite of my cookie than not, so he really didn't have to try this hard. But the fact that he opted to work for it made me feel like he knew he was getting a prime cut. He wasn't taking any chances tonight.

"I'll be right back with your entrees," Jennie said.

Jennie arrived five minutes later with our food. Thank goodness too. I needed something to help soak up all that wine I'd been drinking. But I'm telling you that wine had me feeling nice. I was like a giggling school girl laughing at all of Bernard's jokes and hospital stories. Outside of being sexy as hell, he had a nice sense of humor. I liked that.

The drinks helped me to relax to the point where I felt comfortable in asking Bernard some personal questions.

"Do you have any siblings?" I asked.

He waited until he'd chewed and swallowed his food before saying, "I am one of three children born and raised in California. My sister is a successful realtor in Arizona, and my younger brother passed away from a drug overdose. My mom is still alive and, well, my dad deserted the family for a younger selection during his first year of medical school."

I nodded and was very interested in knowing more. He said that last part with such distain that I immediately knew he must not have been married. I couldn't see him turning around doing to his wife what his father had done to his mother.

"What about nieces and nephews?" I asked.

"Yes. My sister has twin boys. I make it a point to see them every year on their birthday."

The way his eyes lit up when he talked about his nephews, I could tell he liked kids, which led me to my next question?

"What about you? Do you have any children of your

own?"

"No." He shook his head with regret then pushed his plate away. He'd eaten about three fourths of his meal.

I consciously, for the first time, looked at his wedding ring finger. It was bare. "Never found the right woman to marry, huh?" I said, taking a bite of my steak.

"Sure I did. But just because a woman makes a great wife doesn't mean she'll make a great mother. I was looking for a woman like my mother to be the mother of my children." He stared off as if thinking about his mother. "Before my father abandoned us, my mother took excellent care of her home and family. She kept that house spotless, showed up at the schools to make sure we were doing what we were supposed to be doing, and she showed up at the homework. She made sure dinner was prepared every night, laundry was done, and you name it. She ran a tight ship." He paused.

"And then when your father left?"

"She had to go out and work. Two jobs. And on top of that she still did everything she was doing before plus yard work if need be. I mean, my brother and I pitched in, of course, but she wanted us to stay more focused on school, and for my younger brother, his athletics."

"So your younger brother played sports, huh?" Looked like me and Bernard had something in common; brothers who played sports.

"He was the best basketball player I'd ever seen in my life, pro or recreational. But then he got that knee injury." He shook his head. "The doctor prescribed him pain pills. The next thing we knew, my brother was chasing heroine on the streets." He sighed. "Talk about a wasted talent. A wasted life."

Talking about his brother had cast darkness over the atmosphere. I quickly changed the subject. "So do you think you'll ever get married?" I took a sip of my wine.

He shot me a strange look. "I'm married now. Or do you mean will I ever get married again? Because if that's the case, do you know something about my wife that I don't know?" He let out a chuckle.

I, on the other hand, almost spit out the wine that was in my mouth. I hurried up and swallowed it to keep from doing just that. "You're married?" I definitely needed some clarification. I looked at his finger to make sure my eyes had not deceived me. There was no ring.

"Sure. Aren't you?" he shot back. In case I had a problem with his marital status, he was reminding of my own. It was his way of saying that what's good for the goose is good for the gander.

"Well, yes, but you knew that. My husband and daughter were the reason I had to postpone the interview until now. And I thought you said you never found a wife that would make a good mother."

"I did say that." He took a sip of wine nonchalantly and then began topping off his glass. "Hence, the reason why I don't have any children. But my wife, she's fantastic. She's great at being a wife. Wouldn't trade her for the world." He began filling my glass.

It was safe to say that now days, just because someone's finger didn't display a wedding ring didn't mean they weren't married.

"Me and the wife have been together for a few years now. How about you and your husband?" He picked up a forkful of food. I couldn't believe how he was sitting there talking as if I was one of his buddies and we were yapping it up over a beer. "When did you meet?" He placed the food in his mouth, then chewed while he waited on me to respond.

I was still trying to absorb the fact that his man was

married, and was sitting here as casually as ever. I mean, I was too, but my husband didn't happen to be in the same damn city. His wife could walk in any moment and I would have been caught up in some drama.

Not wanting him to think I was bothered, I continued on with the conversation. "My husband was actually my instructor back in medical school."

"Oh, so he was kind of like a school romance."

"Kind of," I said. I'm sorry, but I had to go back to the subject of his wife. My inquiring mind wanted to know. "Is your wife in the medical field as well?"

"No. She's a stay-at-home wife. She was a stay-at-home mother when I met her, but her son is grown now."

I wasn't sure if it was the wine, or if this man was talking in circles. "Now I could have sworn you said that you didn't have any children."

"Of my own."

I shook my head. "Oh, I see. You are one of those men who are literal. You don't lie, but a person has to ask you a million questions to get to the truth. I bet your wife has lots of fun with that." I leaned back in my chair with my glass in hand and took a sip. "Which means that she's probably going to have fun tonight when she questions you about where you were and who you were with."

"What makes you think that? Do you and your husband play those kind of games?"

"Not at all. Truth be told, my husband and I had been estranged up until recently. We decided to try to work things out more so for our daughter than anything else." I'm not sure why I felt the need to play down Dwayne and me rekindling. Sure it might have been solely for Kendra on my end, but somewhere in the midst of it all had been a part of me willing to wholeheartedly give my marriage a try.

"Then why are you having dinner with me?" Bernard asked.

"That question goes both ways. Why are we siting here together and you are not having dinner with your wife? I know why my husband isn't having dinner with me tonight. He's hundreds of miles away."

"I chose to have dinner with you. Don't you think it is proper and in order that I take the newest staff member of the Rainbow OB/GYN unit 12B team out to dinner?"

"Whatever, Bernard, whatever." I shook my head, feeling good and buzzed. The whole thing about learning he had a wife almost messed my buzz up, but it was cool.

You know how some restaurants have bottomless fries, bottomless salad, or bottomless appetizers? Well clearly this place had bottomless wine. It seemed as though the glasses kept filling and filling.

In between the wine, Bernard had him a shot of the green label brand of Jack Daniels. The wine was plenty for me. If I had anything stronger on top of the fountain of wine I'd been sipping from all night, I would have crawled under that table and gave the man a blowjob. That's how twisted I was at this point. The more wine I consumed, the less important my marriage became and the more I wanted Bernard.

My desire to have a sexual encounter that lasted more than ten minutes was long overdue. I couldn't blame Dwayne for not being able to love on me extensively earlier this morning. A quickie was all we could get in considering I had a plane to catch. During water cooler talk I'd heard of men who could get it up and keep it up all night. Unfortunately, I had not encountered such a man in my lifetime. And unfortunately for Bernard, tonight he was going to be the recipient of my sexual desires that this wine was going to see to it were fulfilled.

"You look like you're feeling good over there. You've loosened up quite a bit."

"And hopefully you've stiffened up." I giggled like a silly drunk, because that's exactly what I was at the moment.

Bernard got up and sat next to me on my side of the booth. The alcohol had taken over my entire being, so although I wasn't one for public affection, I didn't resist when Bernard's hand began to caress my inner thigh.

"You're so soft," he leaned in and whispered in my ear as he made his way to my warm pastures. "And wet."

I let out a moan as he massaged my clit through my panties. "I'm so glad you wore this dress."

I closed my eyes and tried to stifle my moan as his fingers danced around the seams of my panties and made their way to my flesh. "Me too. I bought it just for you." I bit my bottom lip in ecstasy.

"Feel what you're doing to me." Bernard took my hand and placed it on his manhood.

I began to massage his erect penis.

"Lift up. I'm sure these are nice," he said, tugging on my panties, "but they're in my way."

I slightly raised my bottom up off the chair so that he could slip them off. The cleaning person was sure to find a surprise after the place closed tonight.

I was no longer stroking his penis, but instead was the one receiving all the pleasure his fingers were providing.

"Denise, I have been waiting to get you alone since I saw you this afternoon," he said even though I had not officially granted him permission to call me by my first name. I guess he figured if he could finger fuck me without asking, at the very least he could call me Denise without asking.

I made up my mind that I was going to allow him to do all the talking. If I dared to speak, one of the moans I'd been stifling would have probably erupted from between my lips and drew all kind of attention our way. I began rocking my hips to let him know not to stop, but that I wanted more. Much more than a finger, but since we were in a public space, I was going to take what I could get.

"I want you to cum, but not here," he said, then removed his hand from my private part.

I shot Bernard a look that said, "What the fuck?" Did he really stop right when I was getting into it?

"Let me join you in your hotel room," he said. "There we can finish what we started."

He had brought me right to the point where I was about to climax and then cut me off like a loose string on a dress. And now I was about to unravel. If letting this man join me back at my hotel room meant he could finish bringing me sexual pleasure, then so be it. He could have told me that I didn't get the job and he could have still taken me back to my hotel room and had his way with me. I needed to release.

"Yes," I said.

"Then allow me to excuse myself. I'll take care of the bill and take care of valet so that they can bring my car around."

I nodded my approval.

He stood and walked away.

I bit on my bottom lip thinking about how once he'd finished taking care of the bill and valet, how he was going to take care of me.

Chapter 13

I looked at my glass of wine that was about one-third full. I didn't want to lose my buzz or my courage, so I downed what was left, hoping it would keep me going until we got back to my hotel room and set things off.

Right after I swallowed the last drop, Bernard returned to the table.

"Are you ready?" he asked. "They should be pulling my car around shortly."

"Yes." I gathered my purse. Bernard extended his hand and helped me to my feet while he retrieved his coat off the nearby coat hook. "My flowers."

"Oh, allow me." Bernard retrieved the roses from the table and then led the way to the exit.

Once we reached the door he stopped. "You don't have a jacket or anything?"

"I wasn't prepared for this cold Cleveland weather. I brought a wrap with me, but I left it back at the hotel. Guess I better get used to these Cleveland winters, huh?"

"No worries. I'll warm you up in a minute here." He turned and opened the door for me.

I followed him out and was sooo glad that the valet had pulled the car up and was standing at the open door. When the valet saw that Bernard now had a plus one, he hurried over to the passenger side and opened my door.

"Thank you," I said as I quickly got inside.

"You in okay, Ma'am?" the valet asked.

"Yes," I assured him as he closed the door.

I rubbed my hands together and blew my warm breath on them. The car wasn't warm inside yet.

I watched as Bernard tipped the valet and then got inside the car. He handed me the flowers. It was too damn cold to sit there and hold some dang on flowers. I put them on the floor, keeping them in place with my feet.

Although I was looking straight ahead as I rubbed my hands together, I could feel Bernard watching me. "Here, take this." He took off the coat he was wearing and gave it to me.

"Oh, God, thank you," I said, taking it without hesitation.

"Now where are you staying?" He put the car in drive.

"Right across the way at the Renaissance."

"Oh, you're just a hop, skip, and a jump away."

And good thing too, considering we'd had quite a bit to drink. Surely we could make it across the street safely.

He pulled off and a minute later we were at my hotel. He entered the parking garage and then searched for a parking spot that wasn't reserved for the handicap, or one of those spots for those plug in electric cars.

"I got another surprise for you," Bernard said as he pulled into a parking spot. He kept the car running, keeping it warm.

"You mean besides these beautiful flowers?" I pulled one from the bouquet and held it to my nose.

I felt Bernard's hand slip around mine and passionately take the rose away from me. He looked down at the roses on the floor that were settled between my legs.

"If it didn't before,"—he looked down at my womanhood—"I bet it smells like a rose now."

I giggled. "You are so good."

"I'm better than good, sweetheart." With the rose in hand,

Bernard used both his hands to cock open my legs. He gently took the full bloomed rose and began rubbing it against my pussy. The petals softly brushed against my hairs. He then put the rose to his nose and inhaled deeply. "Mmm," he moaned as he exhaled. "I don't think I can wait to get you up to your hotel room," he confessed.

"Then what do you want to do?" I asked, gazing into his eyes.

He nodded toward the backseat.

"Bernard, we're not a couple of teenagers in high school at make out point or at the drive-in theatre."

"Then let's pretend we are." He took me by the face. "Tonight let's be the furthest thing from the people we really are. Tomorrow we can face reality, but tonight, let's take the limits off of who we are."

I was convinced this guy had read every romance book ever written and was strategically piecing together every line in order to get me out of my panties. Well it had definitely worked considering my panties were back at Blue Point.

He nodded his head toward the backseat, urging me to be a part of his fantasy.

I was submissive, kicking off my heels and then climbing into the backseat. He immediately joined me, only he cheated. He didn't climb between the seats. He got out of the car and got in through the back door. I have no idea why my grown ass hadn't thought of that. I guess I really was caught up in the fantasy of being a teenage girl again, only this wasn't Granny's basement.

No sooner than Bernard closed the door, his tongue was down my throat.

"Mmm," I moaned at just his touch and the passion of which he was tonguing me down.

He pulled out of the kiss. "Do you want it?" He stared

me in my eyes as he waited on my reply. "The other surprise I have for you." He looked down at his stiff penis.

I was panting like a bitch in heat. And I did mean bitch as in female dog. Did I want it? Hell yeah I wanted it, but I didn't want to seem too desperate, so I simply nodded, hoping that sincerity was bleeding from my eyes.

He then grabbed me by the shoulders and turned me around to face the window. He took charge and I loved every minute of it.

"Tell me how much you want it," he said as he slipped my dress above my ass.

He placed a hard, wet kiss on my left butt cheek. "Tell me," he repeated over and over, slapping my ass a couple times. Even the sound of his hand connecting with my bare skin made me wet.

I could hear him undoing his pants. Next he began to rub his manhood against my pussy. Feeling his flesh on mine almost made me lose it.

"I want it bad." I moaned.

"You are so wet, and so warm and creamy. This alone can make me cum," he said. "But I want to feel the inside of you."

On that note I felt the tip of his penis enter me. It was so fat and thick. I could hear the wetness as he plunged in and out of me. Each time he re-entered me, he slipped more and more of himself inside. He was filling me up the same way he kept filling my wine glass up.

"Does that feel good, baby? Is this enough for you? Sure it is, but let me hear you say it."

Oh, so he was a cocky bastard. He knew he was packing. In case I'd had any preconceived notions about the size of a white man's dick compared to a black man's, he'd knocked it right out of my head with each pump. But he wanted to hear me confirm such. He wanted his ego stroked. Well that was all right by me, because I wanted my pussy stroked.

"It's more than enough," I said. I figured the more I stroked his ego, the more he would stroke my kitten.

"You damn right it's more than enough, and I want you to take it all." He spoke with authority as he slid himself in and out of my pussy, his hips gyrating as if he was churning butter. Slowly but surely he was handling his business.

I wanted to throw my ass back at him so badly, but that might have made him cum quick, and like I said before, I was long overdue for a sexual encounter that lasted longer than ten minutes.

The more he plunged in and out of me, the wetter I got. I felt his hand grab his vessel. He began massaging me with it from my wetness to my ass. I was dripping so much it felt like he was pouring baby oil down my backside. He was lubing every inch of himself, as well as my skin that he rubbed against.

Refraining from slamming myself against him so that I could feel him deeper inside of me, I simply offered moans and groans to let him know that I was enjoying every minute of our encounter. I was enjoying every inch of our encounter.

"This is the only pussy that can handle this entire dick. It fits perfectly. Feel that?" He demonstrated by slowly dipping in and out of me. "I love your fucking cunt."

And that comment right there was the sole reminder that I wasn't dealing with a Black man. Bernard had used the C word. A brotha would have used the P word.

My heart was beating one-hundred beats a minute. The more he talked sexy to me, the louder the moans. Before I even realized it, I felt something entering my womanhood and my anus simultaneously.

"Oh, God!" I called out, never having felt anything like that in my life. I felt opened up. Wide open. At first I didn't know what the hell was going on. It took me a minute to figure out that it was his fingers playing inside my vagina and his penis penetrating my rear. It felt fucking explosive. It looked like tonight I wasn't even going to last five minutes, let alone ten. I'd never experienced anything like this before.

Dwayne had been trying to talk me into having anal sex for years. I just couldn't see how that would ever feel good. Now I was kicking myself, wishing I'd tried it a long time ago. Hell, we may have never separated!

This feeling of being pleased in both orifices at the same time took me to a whole other dimension.

"Oh, yeah, yes," I moaned as I threw my hips back at him. I could no longer refrain. I wasn't going to last too many more minutes, so I no longer cared about whether he came quickly or not.

The smacking sound was like an aphrodisiac. I looked over my shoulder to witness him thrusting inside of me. His hands were gripped around my waist and he was watching intently at himself go in and out of me. I imagined my cream filling being all over his long john.

I felt like I was watching a porn, only I was the porn star in this skin flick. Seeing him do me just right heightened the feeling.

"Fuck," I said, mad that I was about to pour my juices out all over him. I turned back forward, put my head down, and began to tremble.

"That's right. I feel it. I feel you cumming all over me," he boasted. "That's right. Cum, damn it. Cum all over me, because I'm . . . about . . . to-" He couldn't even finish his sentence as he began to tremble right along with me.

"I'm cumming. I'm cumming. Don't stop! Please, don't stop." I was not too proud to beg. I was not too proud to let this man know he was doing the damn thang and that he'd brought me to a climax like no other. "Don't stop." I moaned as I slowly began to come down off of my sexual high.

And he didn't stop. He placed his hands on my hips and pulled me hard against him. Within seconds I could feel his creamy, liquid warmth release inside of me.

"Uhhh, oh shit." I could feel his vessel jerking around in my ocean. "Fuck!" He sounded as if he was mad it was over with as well.

"Oh, yeah," I said as I felt him put in a couple more slow and gentle strokes.

I then heard him exhale as he fell over my back.

We both lay there spent, breathing in and out heavily.

"You know what?" he managed to ask in between breaths.

"What?" I breathed out.

"I think I'm going to love you working under me." He then kissed me on the cheek and said, "Literally."

Chapter 14

I was completely embarrassed to be sitting on the plane barfing in the barf bag, which was pretty much the only free thing airlines offered anymore. I was just glad to be on the plane. I'd forgotten to set the alarm on my phone, but thank God the front desk called me and woke me up, or else I would have missed my flight. No, I hadn't scheduled a wake-up call. Checkout was at 11:00 AM, so at 11:05 AM the front desk called me to ask if I needed a late checkout. That's when I looked at the clock and realized I had overslept.

I jumped out of that bed so quick that my head spun . . . or the room spun. One or the other. It was from a combination of too much wine and the fact that I'd jumped up out of a dead sleep, both which were good for causing headaches. My stomach began to churn, but I didn't even have time to stop and throw up. I'd done my best to hold it down all morning, but as soon as we hit turbulence that was it. The contents of my stomach came up. Not only was it embarrassing to be sitting in between two people and puking, but the vomit wreaked of alcohol, a sure sign that I wasn't sick due to the plane's turbulence, but due to a late night out with the doctor.

Maybe the smell of the alcohol was covering up the smell of sex, because due to the fact that I had been running late, I didn't even have time to hop in the shower. Damn I wish after I'd left Bernard's car and staggered up to my room I would have gone on and gotten my shower out of the way. But the moment I entered my hotel room and saw that bed, I went right for it. That bed had been like a big ole magnet and I was a big strip of metal.

So here I sat smelling of puke and sex. Ugh, I wanted to puke all over again just thinking about it.

"Can I take that for you?" the flight attendant came over and asked me. "And here, I bought you this. It's crackers and ginger ale. It should help settle your stomach."

"Thank you," I said as she and I made the exchange.

Needless to say, the return flight to Norfolk was a very long and certainly not an enjoyable one. Although I had enjoyed the sexual encounter from the night before, the rendezvous lasted clear into the early morning hours. Believe it or not, once we were able to catch our breath, Bernard had the nerve to go down on me. Yes, he still had yet another surprise up his sleeve. You would have thought he was the one trying to get the job.

Let me throw it in there that I owe the good doctor one. In other words, it was a sixty-eight and not a sixty-nine. I was not about to suck his dick after it had been in my ass. Instead I stroked him to sleep, where we both lay snoring in his backseat until his wife called his phone, waking us up. I slowly eased out of the car and waved goodbye while he dealt with his wife.

I kept telling myself that last night was nothing more than a business deal. My job interview and my skills had helped me land the job. The whole little date thing sealed the deal.

If I recalled correctly from the initial job posting, that particular position wasn't slated to begin until early May. That meant I had time to tie up some loose ends at my current job, and most importantly, with Dwayne. I wasn't so sure about moving Kendra for a second time, but I really wanted to be with her. This job, being new and all, was going to be demanding. No room for error or fuck ups. What good would it be to move Kendra all the way here just so she could be in some latchkey program or with some sitter the majority of the time? She might as well stay with Dwayne for that matter.

Although the last thing I wanted to do as a mother was leave my child yet again, I could not allow my selfishness of wanting her to live with me make her miserable and unhappy. I'm sure she'd prefer to be with her father than some strangers while Mommy was out working all day.

There was one thing I hadn't thought about. What if Dwayne ended his contract with Sentara the same as I was doing? That wouldn't even surprise me knowing him and all his goddamn *surprises*. I had to confess; Bernard had better dick and surprises than Dwayne.

Things were more confusing between Dwayne and me than they were back when I'd applied for the job at Rainbow. I was sorry I had agreed to reunite. Just that quickly another man besides my husband had me wide open. That alone should have been my confirmation that I had hung onto this marriage longer than I should have simply because we shared an offspring. Perhaps it was time to call things as they were and keep it moving. And what they were was over.

I know. I know. I wasn't talking all that ying-yang when Dwayne was laying the pipe yesterday morning. But now someone else had laid the pipe, and just a little bit better.

I hated to keep using Kendra as an excuse to stay with Dwayne, but this really would kill her; us teasing her with this false hope of her family getting back together.

"Ugh." I had not meant to say that out loud. The passengers next to me flinched, thinking I was about to puke all over therm.

When I tell you that each of them extended their barf bag

to me so quickly that it wasn't funny, I am not kidding.

"I'm okay. I think I'm going to be fine," I said, turning my head from one passenger to the other.

"You sure?" the passenger on my left asked.

"Yes, I'm sure," I replied to him.

"Here, take mine anyway," the woman on the right insisted.

I took the bag and placed it in the seat pocket in front of me. "Thank you."

"Don't mention it," the woman stated.

I had to admit, thinking about the mess I was in with Dwayne really was about to make me sick to my stomach. But I think I'd already puked as much as I was going to for the day.

I placed my head against my seat and thoughts of my baby girl filled my head. Kendra would be turning seven years old on her next birthday. Both Dwayne and I were trying so hard to keep the family unit together. I was especially divided because I was raised without a father in the home. Our marriage had begun to turn sour about the time Kendra turned four years old. It may have been the stress of Kendra being diagnosed with Sickle Cell Anemia that caused us to begin to drift apart. The doctor in each of us could only focus on her and not each other.

That's when all these constant and uncertain feelings I began to have about Dwayne surfaced. The farther he drifted away from me, the more I wondered is if he was getting closer to someone else. In other words; I wondered if he had a piece on the side. Before then I'd never even thought twice about stepping out on Dwayne. But the more I thought about the possibility that he was cheating on me, the easier it made it for me to cheat on him.

I ended up tucking those uncertainties deep away for a long time. Imagining Dwayne with another woman would only turn me into something I didn't want to be. I was fine as hell and could rock all the latest fashions and slay, but jealousy never looked good on me. So I never questioned my man about his comings and goings or went through his call log. Besides, going through a doctor's call log would be in vain. He could claim every person on the list was a patient, and I wouldn't know any better. Those feelings of uncertainty were not a result of my guilty alter ego. It wasn't an excuse for me stepping out on the marriage. It was me being true to myself about what was going on in my marriage.

The six- month marriage counseling sessions we participated in while we were in Germany were helpful in the beginning. In the first couple of sessions the counselor had us talking about ourselves as individuals. We learned more about one another from those counseling sessions than we had in all our years of marriage. Counseling had been Dwayne's suggestion. That was proof that I wasn't the only one who knew our marriage was like the Titanic. No matter how big and pretty it was, it was a sinking ship.

It was those later counseling sessions where things started to go downhill; the sessions where the counselor wanted us to talk about us as a couple and our marriage. Dwayne's and my marriage was so boring that even our counseling sessions were a snooze. We honestly had nothing we were fighting over. Maybe fighting would have been good. At least we would have been communicating.

The last few sessions we only attended for routine purposes. We each knew in our mind that the marriage had totally fizzled out. I had already made the den area of our home the place where I laid my head. Thank God there was a pullout couch in there.

The counselor had suggested we do some role playing as

homework to spice up our marriage. Awkward and weird is all I can say. We both discontinued the useless task after the couple of assignments. We both agreed that the counseling sessions were not helping our situation. The end result was no more marriage counseling. No more marriage, at least in the traditional sense. So I put in for a job in the States and now here I was.

My eyes snapped open, because in that moment I realized where I was. Literally I was on the plane, but figuratively, I was back on that same old sinking ship. In that instant my phone conversation with my mother popped in my head; the one I never followed up with her on.

"That boy you were in the service with died," my mom had said. *"He was your age."*

I remembered thinking how he'd been too young to die. He hadn't even lived life. I was not going to die knowing I had not lived the life I truly desired to live.

During the remainder of the plane ride back to Norfolk, I mustered up the courage to discuss with Dwayne how I really felt. I couldn't continue on with this game of emotional charades. In the end I didn't see where it would benefit any of us, not even Kendra. She needed her parents to be happy in order for her to be happy. And I was happy when I thought it would just be Kendra coming to join me in Norfolk. I'd only been torn and twisted after finding out Dwayne would be joining her.

I refused to live the rest of my life like this. I could have stayed in Aliquippa if I wanted to be miserable. I'd worked too hard to not enjoy life. It was time to be true to myself. Hell, it was time for Dwayne to be true to himself. Just think; I was blocking some other woman's blessing by agreeing to hang onto something that wasn't there. There was some woman out there who would love Dwayne's dirty boxers. There was a woman who deserved a good man like him. I'm not saying that I didn't deserve a good man; it's just that a good man didn't deserve me, not at this point in my life.

Something told me that Dwayne's feelings were mutual. However, neither one of us would step up to the plate. So many foul balls and strikes had been thrown, yet we both kept overlooking them and continued on with the game without calling the plays exactly what they were. Couples divorced all of the time. Surely they had still somehow managed to raise intelligent, successful, and financially independent children even though they raised them in separate homes.

Although I was very proud of my professional accomplishments, I also knew my heart would carry the many burdens resulting from the "D" word. I loved my husband deeply for all that he'd contributed to my life. In addition to him giving me the most amazing and beautiful daughter in the world, he was partially responsible for me becoming a successful doctor. However, the depths of my emotions were not strong enough to keep me committed to my marriage vows. I desired more. Love was not enough. And being in love, well, that ship had long sailed . . . and sank.

By the time the plane had touched down, my mind was made up. Dwayne's and my marriage being over would be made official when I filed for divorce. And I owed it to him to tell him sooner rather than later.

Chapter 15

When I caught sight of Dwayne's car that he'd had shipped over from Germany, I waved my hand in the air while the other rested on my luggage. I'd just stepped out of the airport doors. Leave it to Dwayne to be prompt and on time. He was always on time; another one of his admirable attributes.

I could see Kendra's little face plastered to the glass in excitement to see her mommy. She looked as if she was so eager to get to me that she was about ready to jump out of the car while it was still moving.

I couldn't help the smile on my face that stretched a mile wide. Kendra was my everything. And in that moment the strangest feeling erupted inside of me. I swear to God it took everything in me not to burst out crying.

What had I done and what was I about to do? I hadn't only been cheating on Dwayne all of this time. I'd been cheating on Kendra. I'd been cheating on my family. I'd been cheating on my damn self. Why didn't I have the balls when I left Dwayne in Germany to actually leave Dwayne in Germany for real? To end this strained relationship we called a marriage? I should have spoken up and made it clear that I wanted out. That it was completely over. Instead I left the door to possibilities open, and Dwayne walked right through it.

Had we both acted like grown-ups and been honest with one another, the initial shock Kendra would have experienced of hearing that her mommy and daddy were no longer going to be together would have worn off by now. But instead she was about to get the shock of her life once we sat her down and broke the news.

"Mommy!"

Once Dwayne pulled over to the curb, Kendra hopped out of the car and came running to me.

"I missed you." She flung her arms around me. "Did you bring me a souvenir?"

"Yeah, did you bring us a souvenir?" Dwayne joked as he got out of the car. "A LeBron James jersey or something?"

As if I hadn't already felt guilty enough inside, here I'd been so caught up in finding the perfect dress for Bernard to screw me in, that I didn't even get Kendra a souvenir while I was at the mall. I always bought her souvenirs, even if I'd already traveled to the location before and had gotten her something.

"You know what, baby? I think I might have left it back at the hotel." Kendra frowned. "But don't worry. I'll call the hotel and have them mail it to me." Since the hotel was connected to the mall, I'd order something online from one of the stores in the mall. It would be as if the souvenir was coming from the hotel. That way, in my mind, I wouldn't be lying to Kendra.

A smile covered her face again.

"Hey, baby. I missed you too." Dwayne walked up to me, put his arm around me, and kissed me on the lips. He took his thumb and pulled my face to his. I looked downward. I couldn't even look him in the eyes. "I'm glad you're home."

I inhaled. He was wearing my favorite cologne, Armani Code by Giorgio Armani.

"I'm glad to be home," was all I responded with. Again, I'd made my mind up not to play games, so I wasn't going to lie and say, "I miss you too."

I psyched myself out by telling myself that today was no different than any other in the past. It was the same old usual stuff to make those on the outside looking in think we had a normal marriage. A peck on the lips, a lame "I miss you," and we were back in the car and on our way.

"You buckled up, lady bug?" I asked Kendra as Dwayne drove off.

"Yep," she said, and then began asking me a million questions about Cleveland.

"Did you see the king while you were in Cleveland, Mommy?"

I looked over my shoulder with a puzzled face. "The king?"

"Yes, King James," she said, giving me that "duh" expression.

"Oh, LeBron." I chuckled and turned back around. "No, but I was in the same building as the arena where he plays basketball. So I guess you could say I was in the king's castle."

"Wow! That's good too."

"Umm, hmm," I agreed.

On and on my little chatterbox went, but I didn't mind at all. It kept me from having to hold a conversation with Dwayne. But halfway home Kendra ran out of things to say. After a few minutes of silence, Dwayne picked up where Kendra left off.

It was our usual conversation that consisted of a day in the life of work at the hospital. *Same ole boring shit,* I thought to myself. But I did notice something that made me feel slightly uneasy. It was the tone in Dwayne's voice. I couldn't put my finger on it, but I could tell something was up. He was talking, but it was as if he was holding back from what was really on his mind. Or maybe he was scared that he'd say too much, but he didn't want to not say anything at all. It was odd, because all at the same time he was saying a lot while trying not to say something.

I wondered if Dwayne, like me, had given our relationship some thought while I was away. Maybe, just maybe he'd come to the same conclusion as I had. But he hadn't spoken up before, so perhaps this was my opportunity to speak up for the both of us.

"Dwayne, we need to talk," I said as we pulled up in our driveway.

He didn't respond right away. He threw the car in park, paused, and then turned and looked at me. "About what?" He exhaled as if the inevitable was coming to pass.

"I'd rather, you know"—I nodded back toward Kendra—"Talk later."

"Well, I have to go into the hospital. I switched shifts so that I could be home with Kendra and be able to get you from the airport."

"Can you meet me when you leave the hospital? Maybe meet me out for dinner?" Just in case our conversation didn't go as civilized as I was hoping, I was opting to talk in a public place.

Dwayne washed his hand down his face.

"I will get a babysitter for Kendra. I'll see if Tracy or her sister can come over to the house."

He looked over at me. "I will try my best. If I'm not mistaken, I think I was scheduled to have dinner with a new colleague tonight. I'll double-check my calendar, and if that's the case, I will try to reschedule the dinner so that I can meet you."

"Thank you. I appreciate it."

Dwayne exited the car while Kendra and I both sat and waited for him to come open our doors. As I watched him walk around the front of the car to let me out first, all I could do was exhale. Step one, "we need to talk," was completed. Now on to step two; the break up.

***

My stomach was in knots as I drove to Byrd & Baldwin Brothers Steakhouse. That's where Dwayne and I had agreed to meet once he cancelled the dinner plans he'd originally had so that he could join me. I was grateful for that. I would have lost my courage overnight if I'd had to wait until tomorrow.

"Oh shit!" I said, slamming on my breaks as it registered in my head that the light I'd been staring at as I approached it was red. Red means stop, but yet I'd kept going the same way my brain was in overdrive and kept going and going.

"Get it together, girl, get it together," I coached myself.

My phone began ringing. It was in my purse instead of my console, so I dug into my purse and answered it while I sat at the red light.

"Hello!" I said, answering it on the last ring before it went to voicemail. This was the reason why I usually placed my phone in the center console once I got into the car. The same way people get distracted from talking and texting while driving, they can have the same fate while digging for the phone itself.

"Well, damn, stranger?"

I immediately recognized the voice on the other end of the phone as Tasha's. "Hey, girl, what's up?"

"Nothing, just wondering why I don't hear from my best friend anymore. How are things going?"

"Fuck my life!" I yelled out.

Tasha laughed. "It's been that bad, huh?"

"Worse."

"Dwayne giving you the blues like that? He seems really cool. I've only bumped into him a couple times since that day you introduced him to me in the hospital cafeteria, but he seems cool."

"He is cool. Cool as hell."

"Then what's the damn, problem, girl? I wish the hell I did have someone who loved my stankin' panties the way that man loves yours."

"The problem is me. I haven't been honest with Dwayne and I haven't been honest with—" The blaring horn coming from the car behind me cut off my words. I looked up to see that the light had turned green—"Myself." I finished my sentence as I drove off. "I don't want to be married. I don't think I ever have, so the last thing I want to do is work on keeping this marriage together."

"Then why didn't you tell the man that from jump? Have him flying all the way from Germany to be with you. You are just wrong. Dead wrong."

"Thank you, bestie. I knew if I called you you'd make me feel so much better," I said sarcastically. "Which explains exactly why I haven't called your ass," I snapped, rolling my eyes as if she could see me.

"Don't be getting snappy with me," Tasha said. "And don't be rolling your eyes either. I know you, so I know that's exactly what you're doing. Like your mama used to say when you used to pull that mess with her . . ."

Tasha and I both repeated my mother's words in unison. "Keep rolling those eyes and they gon' be rolling across the floor when I knock 'em out of your head."

We burst out laughing. It felt good to laugh. I should have called Tasha a long time ago. I needed this. Tasha had been my confidant for years. Even though we'd spent so much time apart, once we reconnected it was as if we hadn't been apart at all. I still felt just as close and trusting of her. And today I was about ready to explode with emotions. Let's just say Tasha's phone call unscrewed the cork, and now I was popping all off at the mouth with my business.

I spoke with Tasha for the remaining ten minutes of my drive to the restaurant, telling her how I was on my way to meet Dwayne to have "the talk" with him. "Well, I'm pulling into the restaurant parking lot now."

"Call me and let me know how things go," Tasha said. "Or if you need me to come help you whoop his ass if he gets all psycho on you and shit. 'Cause you know he has just cause to go psycho. You did make the man fly thousands of miles, ship automobiles, sell off his furniture, and-"

"Good bye, Tasha."

"Don't be mad at me be-" There was a clicking sound as if another call was coming in. "That's the hospital on my other line," Tasha said. "Don't forget to call me."

"I won't," I said before ending the call.

I drove to the restaurant door. I looked down at my watch. It was already 6:30 PM. Dwayne and I were supposed to meet at 6:00 PM. So in my world, of course, I was right on time. I pulled up to valet parking and the attendants greeted me as usual. This was one of my favorite spots to dine, and not only because of the delicious food, but they had tasty candy as well; eye candy. I was especially attracted to the young, cute Black mixed with Korean little young hottie. He often worked on Friday nights when I usually dined alone. I would flirt with him, sometimes even giving him one of those "You want some of this" looks.

He always flirted back, but I think that was so I would leave him the usual ten dollar tip. Everyone else got five.

I got out of the car, took my valet ticket, and after stuffing it down in my purse, made my trek to the restaurant door. I continued to have mixed emotions about the pending breakup meeting with Dwayne. The possibility of the unknown had my stomach in knots.

Even though I'd be taking my job at Cleveland soon, for the next month or so Dwayne and I still had to live together. I'd probably let him keep my place until he could find a place of his own. He may not even want to live with me after tonight. He may not want to look at my face. But even so, we still had to work together at the hospital.

There were a lot of bridges to be crossed, and as I crossed the threshold of the restaurant, I was about to get to one of them.

Once I arrived at the hostess station to check in, I learned that Dwayne had not yet arrived. This was very much out of his character. Even though he knew I would have never made it to the restaurant by six, he still would have been there waiting patiently, on his second drink, by the time I arrived.

I was seated by the hostess, and for the first time ever, I was the one who sat waiting for Dwayne to join me for dinner. I wasn't complaining though. The wait gave me time to consume some liquid courage. Unlike last night, though, one glass of wine would be plenty for me. I had to work in the morning, so I definitely couldn't afford to put myself in a position where I'd be barfing all over the hospital like I had done on the plane.

I was halfway through my glass of wine and an appetizer when I did a search of the restaurant. I thought it was possible that Dwayne could have accidentally been seated elsewhere and that he was sitting around waiting for me. When there was no sign of him, I decided to page him on his hospital pager. There was a great possibility that he could have gotten tied up at the hospital.

When he didn't return my page after a few minutes, I decided to send him a text. I gave him the benefit of doubt that he was probably with a patient, so I didn't bother calling, knowing he wouldn't have been able to answer his phone anyway. If he didn't return my text, though, that would be my next step.

Because Dwayne was always on time or ahead of time, I couldn't say that if he was ever going to be late he usually called. He'd never been late. There was no way he'd forgotten about our dinner plans this evening, especially when he was the one who had called me to let me know it was a go. I was not about to keep tracking this man down, so finally I gave up and decided to enjoy the remainder of my colossal shrimp cocktail appetizer.

"Would you like to go ahead and order your entrée?" my server came over and asked, trying her best not to show how sorry she felt for me that I'd been stood up, but it was written all over her face.

"No entrée," I said, "but could I get a shot of 1800, please?"

She was glad to bring my drink order, of which I wasted no time at all downing, chasing it with the remaining wine in my glass.

"There," I said to myself softly. "That ought to drown the embarrassment of being stood up by my husband." So much for only having a glass of wine.

Even though the entire purpose of this dinner was to let Dwayne know that I wanted a divorce, I was still feeling some kind of way that he was a no-show. I thought about the tone in his voice earlier, and now him not showing up. I didn't know what it was, but something was up.

Thoughts of Dwayne having a little something going on, on the side crept up in my head. As of late, I'd honestly never thought about nor cared whether Dwayne had a side-chick. I don't even know why it was consuming my thoughts, or better yet, why I felt a slight tinge of jealousy. Why should I care, considering I'd spent last evening romping around in the backseat of Bernard's car? I don't know, but for some reason I did. Ironically enough, the fact that I was a cheat is probably why I was thinking the same about Dwayne. Instead of being worried that something bad had happened to him, I was worried that he was out doing something bad to me.

The first four years of Dwayne's and my marriage, I definitely would have had an issue if I found out Dwayne had been unfaithful to me. I cared then. It was not until after our daughter turned four when things seemed to change; when I stopped caring.

It was clear that I was hell-bent on reminding myself why I needed to divorce Dwayne. It looked as though sharing my reasons with him wasn't going to happen tonight.

By the time I'd finished up my shrimp and paid the check, Dwayne still had not arrived nor had he returned my text or pages. I'd even broken down and called him. Still nothing. For the first time, worry was starting to set in instead of jealousy and anger.

After leaving the restaurant, I decided to head over to Tasha's house. She'd been complaining that I'd been neglecting her, plus I needed to vent about being stood up. So why not? Besides, the sitter wouldn't be expecting me for another couple hours.

A few minutes before I got to Tasha's house, my stomach was all torn up in knots. Maybe I should have laid off the alcohol tonight, but it wasn't just the alcohol. I had a weird feeling of anxiety in the pit of my stomach. I could feel the contents of my stomach rising. I quickly pulled over to the side of the road and vomited.

I was so unhappy and miserable that it had made me sick to my stomach.

Afterward I sat parked for a moment with my head leaned back against the headrest. "I just want to be happy," I told myself. "I just want to be fucking happy!" I banged my fists on the steering wheel.

How had my life ended up so confusing? Now here I sat sick with guilt, worry, jealousy, regret, and so many more undesirable emotions. Tears began to spill from my eyes. That only delayed me from continuing on with my drive, because I couldn't see due to my blurred vision caused by the tears.

There was no way I'd be able to see in front of me to drive. My heart was so heavy. Where was Dwayne? Had he been able to see right through me and knew what this dinner meant, which is why he hadn't shown up? Was this his way of avoiding the inevitable? That was my heart talking. My head was saying that maybe he was up to no good the same way I'd been up to no good last night.

My stomach felt as if it was a bottomless pit. I did not know what to think anymore.

Once able to gain my composure, I headed on to Tasha's house. As I turned the corner into her housing development, I spotted a Navy Blue 525i BMW. That was the same kind of car Dwayne drove, which was probably the only reason why I even noticed it in the first place. But it was when I saw the license plate that my heart dropped.

"Dwayne?" his name fell from my lips and shattered in my lap. Why was Dwayne here instead of with me at that restaurant getting broken up with? And who was he here seeing? If he knew what was good for his ass, it better had been an emergency with a patient, because he hadn't lived in Virginia long enough to make any friends that he could be hanging out with.

Many thoughts began to surface in my mind. Should I go beat on all these doors and find my man, or should I simply wait for Dwayne to come home tonight and catch him in a lie? My instincts told me to park somewhere and watch to see which condo he came out of. *Yeah, that's what I'll do,* I told myself, until my urge to have to urinate surfaced. Me and this damn bladder. I really needed to stop drinking so much.

I decided I would just go ahead to Tasha's. She could come back out here with me and stand watch just in case I needed backup. This at least explained what the weird and unusual feeling I had been experiencing was; women's intuition.

It looked as though I'd been nervous all night for nothing. Here I was worried about cutting Dwayne off, and then this son of a bitch goes and hands me the scissors.

I had to drive several condos down in order to get to the one Tasha lived at. Sneaky bastard had no idea my girl even lived out here. He probably figured I'd never find him here in a million years. What were the odds?

Once I got to Tasha's place, there was a black Lexus with Georgia tags parked in her reserved spot, of which I had no idea to whom it belonged. She had a detached garage, so she never used her reserved spot anyway, but her company always did. The one time I was about to piss my pants and needed to hurry up and park so I could go to the bathroom, someone decided to use her space.

"Well damn," I fussed, noticing that the entire lot was pretty full tonight.

All the visitor spots were taken, so I ended up parking in a reserved spot down the way. I hoped I didn't get towed. That was a chance I was going to have to take.

I got out of the car and made my way to Tasha's condo. Her garage door was shut, so I wasn't sure if she was home. She hadn't mentioned whether she had plans or not when I'd talked to her. I pulled out my cell phone to call her, but I was damn near about to piss my pants. Didn't nobody have time for that. I recalled that Tasha always left her side door open. Tonight I would definitely be using it, because if I stood there and waited for her to open the door, I'd find myself standing in a puddle.

As I crept by the garage, I peeked inside the window on the side door. "Yes, she's here," I said upon seeing Tasha's SUV parked inside.

Just as I arrived at her side door, I hesitated, thinking maybe I should call her. What if that Lexus belonged to a little boo thang of hers? Lord knows I wouldn't want to interrupt Stella from getting her groove back. The moment I realized my cell phone was all the way back in my car is when I decided to go ahead and let myself in.

I crept through the door that led to the kitchen. The dim light over the stove was on, which allowed me to see my way through the kitchen and to the half bath that was right off the kitchen.

"Oooh yeah, that's it. Yes!" I heard Tasha yell out. Her voice sounded as if it was coming from her den that doubled as a computer room farther down the hall.

"Oh shit," I whispered to myself.

Looked as though I'd interrupted Tasha getting hers in. Good. She needed someone to help her get over Clarence's ass after all these years. In addition to not only being a good lay, I hoped he was a good man period. Tasha deserved to be with a good man.

I was into a lot of things, but I wasn't into threesomes, so I wasn't about to hang around and disturb Tasha with my issues. But a bitch had to pee like a race horse, so I decided that I would use the facilities before heading out. Although I was in straight Thelma and Louise mode, I'd have to make my task of being on watch for Dwayne a solo adventure. If anything jumped off, I'd be prepared. Beyoncé might have had hot sauce in her bag, but I had pepper spray in mine, and I was willing to use it if need be.

Thank God I only had to go number one, because I was too afraid to flush the toilet after I finished using it, so I threw my toilet paper in the trash, turned the water on lightly, washed my hands, and then exited Tasha's condo the same way I'd entered it. She'd never know I was even there.

I returned to my car and sat for a half hour. Dwayne's car was still in view from where I was parked. Because he had no idea where Tasha lived, he wouldn't even think to look down here. But if I moved my car closer to his, he might look out the window from whatever condo he was in, see me waiting, and then decide to stay hemmed up where he was at.

It was very likely that he would try to wait it out, but this was one standoff he was going to lose, because I wasn't going anywhere until I got to the bottom of things.

I wanted to call Tasha so bad, but she still had company because I hadn't seen anyone exit her place. I called Tracy, but she was pre-occupied with a dinner date, which is the reason why she hadn't been able to sit with Kendra herself versus her sister. Ain't that a bitch? Everybody had a little date for the night, but I'd been stood up; the married one!

After about another half hour, I was getting antsy and more pissed by the minute. I needed to get home to relieve Tracy's sister of her babysitting duties, but I needed to catch Dwayne in the act so that there was no excuse he could possibly make. Eyes didn't lie. I needed Tasha to be my eyes. I hated to interrupt her little date, but this was a serious matter, and surely the two weren't still fucking. If ole boy was handling his business like that, then maybe that was one threesome I did want to be a part of.

I got out of the car and went back to Tasha's side door. I was so nervous about busting in on her like this. Maybe I'd at least creep back in just to make sure they were done doing the do. If I interrupted her with a knock, that would piss her off and make her less likely to want to help me out.

My hands were trembling like that of a patient with Tourette syndrome as I reached for the doorknob. Did I really need to bring Tasha into my mess? My every intention was to be done with Dwayne tonight, so why was I tripping? But I knew deep down inside I would not have been able to rest without knowing the truth. Besides, catching him in the act of infidelity would result in an uncontested divorce for sure. I didn't foresee Dwayne contesting the divorce, but it never hurt to have a little surety.

I entered the condo and gently closed the door behind me. It was very quiet. I didn't hear Tasha's soprano skills either. I crept until I heard the voices coming from the den again. I took a step toward the room and the heels of my shoes began to make their own rhythm. I walked on my tiptoes as I followed the sound of the voices. Lord have mercy, I hope Tasha didn't think I was into voyeurism. My heart was beating so fast that I wanted to abort mission. This wasn't worth it. I was about to make a fool out of myself, and probably embarrass myself in front of whomever Tasha's friend was.

I turned around and headed back to the door.

"Woman, you are too much," I heard Tasha's company say with a chuckle.

The familiar voice stopped me in my tracks. Was that who I thought it was?

Chapter 16

If I thought my heart was beating fast before, it was damn near about to beat out of my chest. I became ice cold inside. I felt as if my warm blood had literally drained from my body. Although I stood there feeling like a Popsicle in a freezer, beads of sweat formed on my head.

I began taking small, short breaths. I inhaled and exhaled quickly. I sure could have used a brown paper bag.

I willed my body to turn back around and finish my trek to the computer room, but it wouldn't move. I couldn't move. My face began to warm, but that's only because of the heated tears that began to stream down my face. They were tears of hurt, pain, and betrayal.

In this moment I felt like I was in one of those nightmares where I was trying to run from something, but my feet wouldn't move, only in this scenario I actually wanted to run to something.

After a few more deep breaths I got myself together. I forced my body to turn back toward the computer room. That was a start, now all I had to do was get my feet to begin to take steps.

Left, right, left, right left, I began. With each step I gained more and more strength. I could do this. It sounded as if my camping out in front of Tasha's condo hadn't ended up in vain after all.

"Here, let me do it," Tasha said.

"If you could handle it yourself, then I wouldn't be here, now would I?"

I heard the voice of Tasha's company again. This time I was closer. This time I was sure.

My body went numb. I began to experience a warm throbbing sensation in my hands. I felt an instant headache coming on. As I approached the halfway open door, I took another deep breath and then clinched my eyes closed in an attempt to lock the tears in.

Any cool, calm, and collectiveness that had once been in my body was exorcised out.

"You dirty bitch!" I yelled, then the next thing I knew I was charging after Tasha like a bull.

Tasha screamed, but that's all she could do. I'd caught her off guard.

"Denise, wait, hold up," Dwayne said as he attempted to pull me off of her, but it was to no avail. I was in a trance and commenced to whopping that ass.

"Stop it!" Dwayne, said, grabbing me by the waist. He had me up in the air, but I had a death grip on Tasha's hair. With this newfound strength I had, I damn near tried to pull her hair off her fucking scalp.

"Denise, what are you doing?" Tasha cried out.

"What the fuck are you doing?" I shot back.

"Please, just stop it! Stop it!" Dwayne said. "If you don't let her go, Denise, I'm going to have to call the police. You're going to kill her."

No this muthafucka didn't. His words instantaneously made me release Tasha's hair, and she went sailing toward the desk she'd been standing at when I'd entered the room. Dwayne had been sitting in the chair at the desk. I don't know if she'd just gotten up from straddling him or what. They didn't appear to be in any type of sexual position, but I didn't care. I know what the fuck I'd heard earlier. I know what I'd heard only a few moments ago. Regardless, these two had no business being together.

I'd spoken to both their asses and not one of them had mentioned meeting up with the other. That alone was a red flag. The only reason why you don't tell someone something is because you don't want them to know. Why would my best friend and my husband keep this from me unless they didn't want me to know? And why didn't they want me to know? What exactly didn't they want me to know?

"Okay, okay," I said to Dwayne. "I let her go. I let her go." I held my hands out in defense, hoping Dwayne would release me.

"You cool?" he asked me for confirmation.

Breathing heavily in between breaths I let him know that I was good.

Slowly, Dwayne let me down, and before he even knew what hit him, my knee was in his groin and I was wind milling the shit out of him. I could hear my arms cutting the air. That's how hard and fast I was going in on him.

He couldn't even fight me back because he was hunched over in complete pain, looking as if he was turning blue. Hopefully I'd kneed him so hard his balls were up in his throat.

I was done. Out of my mind. I had completely snapped. Seeing him and Tasha together made something inside of me click. I pictured all the nasty things Bernard and I had done the night before, and then I imagined the two of them having done the same things. I don't know what all they had done or hadn't done. I was in kick-ass-now-and-ask-questions-later mode.

I'm one of those people who thinks that if a woman's man steps out on her, then it's her man she should be mad at.

It's her man's head she should want to go upside of, but in this case it was different.

Tasha was my day one. She knew more about me than I'd ever shared with Dwayne. I could go through ten husbands in my lifetime, but there was only one Tasha, my true ride or die. One bestie. One person who had been in my life since puberty and knew me as well as I knew myself. The one person who I shared all my life secrets with, and vice versa. But who knew Tasha had a secret she'd been keeping from me?

I never imagined in a million years she would ever betray me like this, which is why I never thought for one second when I saw Dwayne's car that I'd find him at my best friend's place. It absolutely never crossed my mind. That's how much I trusted her. I don't put shit past a man, but her I trusted. How could I have been so wrong? How!?

I hated both my cheating husband and the mistress, who happened to be my best friend. With that being said, both of them were going to get it.

"Stop it! Stop it!" Dwayne said, managing to grab hold of my arms. He quickly spun me around, grabbing my arms and wrapping them around me as if using them as a straitjacket. My back was pinned against his chest and I was staring Tasha dead in the eyes.

"You bitch!" I spat. "I can't believe you did this to me."

"Denise, please. I didn't do anything to you," Tasha said. "I didn't do anything with your husband. It's not-"

"I know you better not say that corny as shit about this not being what it looks like," I warned her. "You had me on the phone telling you I was about to meet up with Dwayne when all the while you knew he was on his way here. He was probably already here."

The thought of her standing there on the phone talking to me with her leg cocked up in the air while my man ate her pussy sent rage through my bones. I wanted to get at her again. Like a Pitbull, I could taste her blood, and once I got a taste of it, I was gon' lock down on that bitch, mauling her until she met an early and violent death.

"Will you listen to me, please? Let me explain." Tasha paused, maybe to see if I was going to allow her to explain. But I didn't need an explanation. I knew what I'd heard and I damn sure knew what I'd seen; what I was still seeing, which was my man all up in my best friend's place.

From what I surmised, while Tasha stood there looking at me all crazy, the wheels were churning in her head, trying to make up a price for something she thought I would buy. Or maybe she was too nervous and scared to locate the truth.

"Dwayne was just . . . he uh . . . well, I uh." I could figuratively see the lightbulb going off in her head as the words she'd been searching for popped up. "I forgot to log some things at the hospital. I could lose my job for it. You know that, so I panicked. Dwayne was only helping me try to figure out how to get in the system."

"Hoe, please! Dwayne ain't been working at that hospital but a month of Sundays. How the fuck he know how to get into the system?"

"She's telling the truth," Dwayne said. "I was helping her try to reboot and re-enter the system with my code because she got locked out after so many failed attempts using her own."

"Don't try to play me stupid," I snapped, because I knew that was a lie. Allowing someone else to log in using our personal passcode, which was like our digital footprint in the hospital, was grounds for termination. "Why would you jeopardize your career?" I asked Dwayne. "Why would you risk your job to save hers? You'd only do that for someone you're married to or someone you're fucking. So since we both know that you're married to me, then you must be fucking her."

"I was just trying to help out *your* friend." Dwayne said it as if he was lightweight trying to blame me. As if I was the one at fault here. What the fuck? Like since Tasha was my friend and his dick fell in her pussy it was my fault. Really?

"Do you wanna see for yourself?" He nodded toward the computer screen.

I didn't even bother looking in the direction of the screen. "I don't care what's on that computer screen," I said to Dwayne and then spoke to Tasha. "If Dwayne was only here to help you out, why didn't either one of you mention it? I'd talked to both of you."

Tasha opened her mouth but no words came out. She looked past me to Dwayne, her eyes pleading with him to jump in anytime and help out.

"See!" I said to Tasha. "You don't even believe the lie you're trying to tell me yourself."

"I'm not trying to lie," Tasha said. "It's just that you're tripping and I'm trying to keep it together and not say the wrong thing to be misconstrued."

"You mean you're trying to not tell the truth," I shot back and let out a sarcastic laugh. "Y'all know what?" I said to Tasha and Dwayne, but could only look at Tasha since Dwayne still had me in a bear hug. "Don't even worry about it, because if you thought you might lose your job for forgetting to fill out a report or whatever, you damn sure gonna lose your job when the hospital finds out you're sleeping with another doctor's husband who also happens to be a doctor at Sentara. You think they are going to allow that Jerry Springer shit up in there?"

"Please, Niecy. Before you go running to human resources and actually risking all of our livelihoods, will you just listen to me?" Tasha pleaded with me as tears ran down her face.

I'm not sure if she was crying because she felt bad for getting caught with my husband, that she'd gotten caught with my husband period, or because I had handfuls of her hair in my fists. Maybe the thought of her losing her job had brought her to tears. Was she in emotional pain or physical pain? I didn't know and I didn't care. All I cared about was my own pain.

"I did listen to you," I spat, trying my best to free myself from Dwayne's clutch. "I listened to you fucking my husband. I was here earlier when you two were in here screwing." I began mocking what I'd heard the first time I'd entered the condo. "Oooh yeah, that's it. Yes!" I said. "That's right, Tasha. I heard yo' ass. Only I didn't know it was Dwayne you were in here with. I left, not wanting to interrupt you." I shook my head. "So I go stakeout the parking lot because I'd seen Dwayne's car parked a ways down, never thinking for one minute he would be in here with my best friend. That's how much I loved and trusted you. And just think, I was coming back in here to solicit your help to watch for the trick he was with. And now I'm finding out you are the trick!" I balled my fists and kept myself from attempting to charge at Tasha again.

"He was only parked far because there are no spaces," Tasha said. "My neighbor's mother passed and friends and family from Georgia are in town."

"She's telling the truth, Denise," Dwayne started to say.

"And you shut the fuck up!" I yelled at him. Did he really think I would believe her if he cosigned? "Got my ass sitting up in that restaurant looking like a fool." I then said to Tasha, "And you knew I was on my way to the restaurant to meet him. Guess you two figured you wouldn't get caught by me since you knew exactly where I was going to be. Talk about a sitting duck." I turned my head over my shoulder. "You got our daughter sitting with a babysitter so you can go get your dick wet."

"This wasn't how this evening was supposed to happen," Dwayne said apologetically. "When one of the nurses on my team at the hospital called me and asked me could I do one of her friends' a favor, I had no idea it was Tasha. She gave me the address and-"

"One thing led to another." I finished Dwayne's sentence for him.

"Damn it, Denise, will you fucking listen?"

I was truly taken aback, because Dwayne never snapped and cussed at me . . . ever. So for him to decide to do it now, when he was the one in the wrong, blew my mind.

"This is my first time ever coming to Tasha's condo," Dwayne said.

"Oh, I get it," I said. "The first time it's always just a mistake. Cool. I can live with that. But had I not caught your ass, I'm sure there would have been a second time. And the second time is a choice, motherfucker." I'd been pretty still in Dwayne's arms up to that point, but a rage filled my body, allowing me to burst out of his hold.

I turned into a wild woman. I leaped for Tasha, but she dashed out of the way before I could get to her, causing me to slam against her desk. I lost it, picking up her computer and throwing it at the window. The computer didn't go through the window thanks to the screen, but the corner of it ripped the screen after shattering the glass in the window.

If I couldn't fuck them up with my bare hands, then I'd tear her condo up.

The bad part about it was that I was confined to just that room because Dwayne stood blocking the doorway. Tasha's punk ass had slithered out of the room. So that den got the brunt of all of my anger. I wish I could have destroyed her entire place the way they'd destroyed my entire heart, but that room alone would have to suffice.

By the time Hurricane Niecy ran through there, that den looked as if a cyclone had it. I'm not sure how long I'd been in there destroying it, or how many times Dwayne had pleaded with me to stop. I don't even know how long I'd heard the sirens in the background until it dawned on me that those sirens were there for me.

It was almost like that feeling of driving tipsy—not drunk, but just a little tipsy—and the minute you see those flashing lights in your rearview mirror and hear that siren, your ass sobers up real quick. Well, that moment was happening now. It took the sounds of the police sirens registering for me to snap back to reality. That shit about temporary insanity was true. I had experienced it firsthand. As I looked around and assessed the damage of the room, I realized it was something that only an insane person could do.

"In there officer," I heard Tasha's voice say in a panic.

I can't even believe that bitch was from the same projects as me. It was an unspoken code that we didn't call the police on each other. We duked that shit out. I guess now that we were grown and not teenagers, that code was no longer a decree.

Once the police entered the room, I did not have any strength left in my body. I had broken out all of the windows in the room. Any and everything I had the strength to pick up was tossed around here, there, and everywhere.

No words were spoken and no questions were asked. The police stormed into the room and immediately slammed me down onto the floor and handcuffed me. Everything began to happen in slow motion. I remember them lifting me up off the ground and roughly escorting me out of the condo in handcuffs. As they led me to the front door and not the side door I had used to enter, I saw Dwayne comforting his lover and my best friend. They stood off in a corner on the opposite side of the room. Tasha's head was buried in his chest. She didn't dare make eye contact with me. Dwayne, on the other hand, locked eyes with me and his eyes followed me all the way out the door. He was shaking his head as if he was disgusted with me. Leave it to a cheating bastard to make his wife feel like it's her fault. We never broke our stare until I was led through the doorway.

After my rights had been read, the Norfolk police drove me out of the condo community. Not even in that moment did I realize the severity of things. I was riding in the back of a police car. But it really hit me how much trouble I was in when I was removed from the back of the car and led into the county jail. I may have lost my mind before while at Tasha's condo, but now I was about to lose my freedom . . . and my mind all over again.

Chapter 17

My eyes opened to a tan ceiling. My body was still as I
tried to figure out where I was. Where had I been the
last time I closed my eyes? I couldn't remember, but what
I did know was that I had a throbbing headache. I went to
reach for my head to massage it, but I couldn't move my arm.
I tried it again, still to no avail. This time I tried using the
opposite arm. That one wouldn't move either. Finally I lifted
my head up and looked down to find my hands cuffed to each
side of the bed.

In a panic my eyes began to dart around the room.
What the hell? I merely thought those words at first,
then I shouted them. "What the hell is this? Where am I?
Somebody help me! Help me please," I began to yell.

Within moments a woman wearing a nurse's uniform
entered the room. "Dr. Simpson, calm down. Calm down."

Easy for her to say. This feeling of being constrained put
a fear inside of me. I was helpless.

"Just relax, Dr. Simpson. It's me, Nurse Durum."

I looked into her big blue eyes that seemed honored
to know me. Well, there was no honor in my lying there
strapped to a bed. All the while I was trying to figure out
exactly where I knew her from, and then it hit me. I'd seen
her around the hospital.

The hospital?

I instantly began looking around the room again. I recognized the wallpaper, the furniture, and the make and model of the television. I looked up again, realizing that I even recognized the ceiling. I was at Sentara hospital, my place of employment. And since I wasn't the least bit pregnant, you can best believe I wasn't in an OB/GYN unit delivery room.

"Where am I?" I asked Nurse Durum, knowing part of the answer.

"You're here at Sentara. Do you know what Sentara is?" she asked.

"Yes," I told her. "What floor am I on?"

She cleared her throat and looked downward. "You're on the lower level."

That was also known as LL. It wasn't the LL I loved back when I was high school. Back then LL stood for Ladies Love, Cool J of course. The LL Nurse Durum was referring to was Lower Level, which was the . . .

"Psyche Unit," Nurse Durum confirmed. "Apparently you had some type of mental breakdown a couple nights ago when they were trying to process you into j-"

"A couple nights?" I asked. I'd actually been in this place for two nights without knowing it? "But . . ." I said, my words trailing off as I tried to recall some things. Where was the last place I remembered being? It was at Tasha's. "Tasha," the word fell off my lips." That's when things started coming back to me. I remembered Dwayne being at Tasha's and me completely losing it, demolishing a single room in her condo that I'd been confined to. At least I think I'd been confined to it. I remember Dwayne blocking the doorway or something like that.

Next I recalled the police intervening and carting me off the jail. That's it. That's all I could recall. So why wasn't

I in jail? Why was I in a hospital, in the Psyche Unit no less? Where were the, "Police?" The word fell off my lips as I looked toward the doorway and noticed the uniformed officer standing outside of my door. He was looking into the room with concern, as if making sure I didn't do to the hospital room what I'd done to Tasha's den.

"You've been highly sedated," Nurse Durum informed me. "Last night we started slowly decreasing your meds."

I heard her, but my eyes were on the officer.

I guess she noticed where my concern was at, because next she said, "Dr. Simpson, you are in the custody of the Norfolk County Jail. They brought you here after not being able to calm you down."

I turned to face the nurse. I swallowed, trying to moisten my dry throat. "Do I, do I have to go back to jail?"

She nodded. "Unfortunately so. But first we want to make sure you're okay to leave the hospital and function. We wouldn't want you hurting anyone, especially yourself."

I swallowed once again. "Visitors. Have I had any visitors?"

"You mean like your attorney or someone?" Nurse Durum asked without waiting for me to answer. "No."

"Regular visitors," I said. "Family? Friends?" I'm not sure who I expected to visit me. At a time like this I would have wanted at least my best friend by my side. But Tasha was the last person I expected to visit me, next to Dwayne of course.

Nurse Durum shook her head. "No visitors. But we have received phone calls from a male inquiring about your condition. I think it may have been your husband."

Dirty bastard, I thought. He's worried about my condition, the one I wouldn't be in if it wasn't for his ass. I refused to spend my brain energy thinking about Dwayne. If it wasn't the case before, it was certainly the case now that as soon as I was free, I was filing for divorce. Hopefully he'd save me the trouble and file it himself. That way Kendra and I-

"Kendra!" I blurted out as thoughts of my baby girl entered my mind.

"I'm sorry, who?" the nurse asked.

I ignored her as I thought of my baby girl's whereabouts. I'd left her with Tracy's sister at my house. Where was she now? Was she okay? My heart was beating fast and I was breathing heavily. I had to calm myself down before I had an anxiety attack.

I knew within my heart that although Dwayne may have been a lousy husband, he was a wonderful father. I was certain that Kendra was being well cared for. But what I didn't know was what all Dwayne had told her. Did my baby girl know that her mommy had been arrested and sent to jail?

"I've gotta get out of here," I told the nurse as I began wriggling my wrist in an attempt to free myself. "My daughter. I have to talk to my daughter and explain . . ." My voice cracked and my eyes filled with tears. The thought alone of having to explain this to my daughter, the little girl who looked up to me, broke my heart.

As if my brain wasn't already in overdrive, I then began to think of my new job opportunity in Cleveland. What was I being charged with? Was it a felony or misdemeanor? A misdemeanor I could possibly beat, but a felony might be harder to fight and a little bit more difficult to keep under wraps.

But then there was the issue of me being admitted to the psyche ward. If this got back to Bernard, I don't care how good he thought the pussy was, there was no way he was going to hire me. Him knowingly hiring someone who had been admitted to the psyche ward was like asking for a malpractice suit if anything was to ever pop off.

I was going to try my best to cooperate and keep things tightlipped. I wasn't even going to request my one phone call when I went back to jail. The fewer people who knew about my predicament, the better.

My job here at Sentara was probably as good as over. But Rainbow didn't have a reason to reach out to them again. For all Rainbow knew, I'd simply turned in my resignation and was moving on. Then of course there was the HIPPA, Health Insurance Portability and Accountability Act. That could protect my medical records, but any legal issues would be public record. I could not allow this to put a permanent blemish on my career. I would do everything possible to make sure I became a resident of Ohio, leaving all this drama in Virginia behind. I would not throw in the towel. I would continue with my game plan, which meant calming down, and talking to this nurse like I had some sense before they really did think I was a nutcase.

After talking with the nurse, she called for the doctor and then took my vitals. It wasn't but about forty minutes later when I heard my hospital door open. I'd dozed off to sleep by then, my head facing away from the door. The opening of the door and then the words from the baritone voice that followed woke me up.

"Dr. Simpson, are you awake?" I heard a male voice ask. "I'm Dr. Cannon."

I fluttered my eyes to get my vison clear. It was show time. I had to make sure this doctor knew I had good sense so that I could get the hell out of this hospital, face my legal woes, and get on with my life.

"Yes," I said, clearing my throat, and then turning to face the doctor. His back was to me, as he'd turned away from me to close the door behind him.

"Good," he said. "Because Nurse Durum told me you were. I'd like to talk with you for a moment if you're up to it."

When the doctor turned back to face me, I know I stopped breathing, so in all actuality, a hospital was right where I needed to be. I needed an AED, Automated External Defibrillator, stat!

"Dr. Simpson, are you okay?" he asked with concern, stepping toward me.

I swallowed hard, reminding myself that I really needed to keep it together. I know a little over a couple months ago, on my elevator ride, I really wanted to meet this man, but let me be very clear; this is not how I anticipated our official introduction taking place.

"I'm Dr. Roland Cannon."

At least now I knew what the 'R' in 'RC' stood for. And I definitely knew what unit he worked in.

I'm not sure if he remembered me or not. If he did, he never let on, as he pulled up a chair next to the bed.

There was no way I was going to remind him who I was. Besides that, hooking up with a man, especially another damn doctor, was the last thing on my mind. I was going to play my role as the good patient and be on my merry way . . . hopefully.

"I want to ask you a few questions, Dr. Sim-"

"Please, call me Denise." I didn't need the constant reminder that this man was a colleague at the hospital I worked at.

Dr. Cannon began asking me a million and one questions in order to evaluate my mental state. I gave him straight-laced, honest answers. There was no acting involved. I was not crazy and didn't belong in a damn psyche ward. I didn't even belong in jail. Tasha got what she deserved. I knew better than to express a lack of remorse.

Back at Tasha's I had truly suffered from an episode of being outside my normally sane mind, but I was back. I proved that to Dr. Cannon with the responses I gave to his questions, because early the next morning I was discharged from the hospital and released back into the custody of the police.

I soon learned that jail was the worst of two evils. I'd take the lower level of Sentara over jail any day. But this wasn't just any day. It was today, and if I didn't stay strong and play my cards right, I could mess up real bad and have tomorrow be just another day; another day jailed. I refused to let that thought get me down. I was going to get out of this place. My tomorrow couldn't be just another day. My yesterdays had been unhappy and disturbed. My tomorrow needed to be one with joy and happiness. My tomorrow had to be a new day, both literally and figuratively. It had to be the start of my new beginning.

So here I found myself in an eight foot by ten temporary home. I had no sense of time, but I could tell it was evening based on the meals that they'd tried to serve me. I had refused every last one of them. I didn't have an appetite. No way could I go from eating shrimp to shit. Even the psyche ward's food had been better than what they were serving here.

I'd been notified that I was scheduled to stand before the magistrate in the morning for a preliminary hearing. *Lord, get me through to the morning.*

All I wanted to do was get through the day. Get through the night, because for now, unfortunately, today was, in fact, just another day . . . locked up.

Chapter 18

I could see the rising sunlight through the small manmade window. I estimated it to be around 6:30 AM. My buttocks were sore from sitting on the ground of my cell. That's where I'd fallen asleep; sitting on the ground, my knees to my chest, with my arms wrapped around my legs.

I couldn't bring myself to sleep in that sorry excuse for a bed. You know it's bad when I'd rather sleep on the ground than on the bed.

Unlike the psyche ward, there was no janitorial staff that came to make sure the place was sanitary. I'd imagined the many women that had lain on that bed before me. I'm sure there were remnants of their dead skin and bodily fluids. I would have woken up with whelps all over my body from scratching off the imaginary and not so imaginary heebie jeebies.

I laid my legs flat in front of me and placed my hand on my belly. My stomach was queasy. I ran my tongue across the roof of my mouth. I thought it might stay stuck there. It felt like a thick film was layering the roof of my mouth. I let out a yawn, which only made my stomach feel that much queasier because my breath smelled like rotten eggs. I desperately desired my battery operated spin toothbrush, Crest toothpaste, dental floss, Listerine mouthwash, and a hot, long bath. With all of the above being out of the question, I settled to work with the small, silver basin next to the commode and all that it had to offer.

My comfy bed back at my place and my marble stone shower were merely memories in my head, certainly not my current reality. Hopefully after having my day in court, all of that would change.

"Chow!" a guard yelled as she carried a tray of food to me.

"Not hungry," I shot before she could even waste her time trying to give it to me.

"What, you going on a hunger strike or something?" She let out a snorting laugh. "Good luck with that."

I forced myself to stand after the guard left. My body was stiff and my bones cracked from not having been mobile for so long. Although it hurt to move, I had to get ready for my hearing today.

After my birdbath, filling my mouth with water and using my finger to scrape my teeth, I put a two-strand twist down each side of my head. I refused to put French braids, corn rolls, or anything that could be mistaken as jailhouse braids on my head.

Once I finished doing my hair, I gave myself a onceover in the mirror. Even the two-strand twists weren't too far of a cry from jailhouse braids, but I had no other options. My hair was a hot mess. It had damn near matted to my scalp after sleeping on it for two days straight. I missed my satin cap; the small things in life I'd taken for granted. I did the best I could do with these naps.

Standing there looking at my reflection in the makeshift mirror that didn't look like much more than a piece of aluminum foil at a barbeque, I had to pinch myself to ensure I was not having a bad dream. It sure did feel like a nightmare.

"Ouch!" Yes, I'd really pinched myself, hard. And no, this

wasn't a nightmare.

"Court!" This time a different guard appeared outside my cell. I heard the guard unlocking my cell as I gave myself one last look. I didn't look much like a well-respected physician, but I damn sure was going to play the part of one.

I was surprised when the guard led me to a small room with teal painted walls. I was even more surprised that there was someone waiting there to see me.

"Hi, Dr. Simpson?" The woman stood from the black, metal folding chair. She held a folder in her right hand.

"Yes," I said, looking her up and down. She looked young. Cute, but young. She wore her thirty-two inch weave like she was a Black Cher. The evenly clipped ends flirted with her buttocks. Her eyebrows were drawn in to just the right thickness to complement her oblong face. She'd worn the mid-price suit as not to appear too flashy, but those shoes gave her away. They were the $300 Tory Burch Gemini Link Bow Leather pumps in black. I'd seen them one day while window shopping in Neiman Marcus. If those were her slummin' it work shoes, then I could only imagine what her girls' night out shoes cost.

"I'm Catara Lambert." She extended her left hand.

There was an impression of what was probably no less than a four carat diamond on her ring finger. Very wise of her to take that thing off before coming here. But again, the one carat stud earrings that had so much clarity I could almost see through them was a dead give-away. This bitch came from M-O-N-E-Y!

"Hi," I greeted, shaking her hand.

"I'm going to represent you today in court." She extended the folder toward the empty chair across from the one she'd been seated at. "Please sit. I'd like to go over some things with you before you go before the judge."

I sat down, trying to figure this situation out. She did not look like a public defender. I did not have an attorney on retainer, so I couldn't determine how it had come about that she was representing me.

"You called me doctor?" I spoke the thought that had popped into my head. I wasn't one hundred percent certain because I'd never been to jail before nor did I roll with jailbirds, but I always thought that once a person was arrested, all of the LMNOPs after their last name were left outside the jail. "How did you know I'm a doctor?" There was a sudden familiarity as I stared at her, waiting for her to respond. "Have we met before?"

"Not formally," she said as she flipped through the file, no longer making eye contact with me at this point. "I was with my sister a few months ago at Sentara Hospital." She spoke nonchalantly. "You introduced yourself as the GYN on staff for that particular day." I was both very proud and impressed to have a Black, female doctor deliver my niece. I admire sisters like myself out here trying to make it. And it just so happened that I was due for some pro bono work my firm requires its attorneys to engage in every couple years. I have a friend at the station who ran off some recent arrests to me. Low and behold I recognized your name."

"I guess now I'm more confused than ever. Seems like the last thing you would want to do is help someone who went from making you proud to be a Black woman, to someone making you look bad as a Black woman."

She stopped reading the file and looked up at me. "First of all, not every Black woman represents me. I have to give another Black woman permission to represent me. Secondly, as a Black woman—who society loves to label as the angry Black woman—I understand that behind every angry Black woman is a man who made her that way. And from what I read in your file, your husband is the loser who made you that way. The Black man makes us angry, then runs off with the happy white chick. Go figure."

I couldn't help but laugh, even though her facial expressions were as serious as could be.

She watched me laugh with her stoic face before a chuckle was able to escape from her lips. "I'm serious," she said. "You had a bad day because, according to what you told the police, you have a bad husband. I can pardon you for that. But now let's see if we can get the judge to." She winked.

I liked this chick right here. She was exactly who I needed to help me get out of the messy bed I'd made.

I was grateful to be in the company of a levelheaded female of authority in the legal system. I could have had some ghetto fabulous trick from the hood that was on a power struggle. Or even one of those parents of pregnant teenagers from months past that I'd dismissed during my professional career. That karma definitely would have been named Bitch.

Catara went over a couple things with me regarding what was about to take place, then the guard came in and interrupted to escort me to court. Catara expressed her good wishes and told me that she was confident everything would work in my favor.

"Thank you," I said, full of her contagious confidence. She was one bad ass sister indeed. She made me want to do right in the name of every Black woman out there. Never again was I going to allow a man to make me end up in a predicament like this . . . or a best friend.

"I'll see you in the courtroom," she said as we were separated.

I was taken to the courthouse in a van along with other inmates. We were placed in a room while we waited for our cases to be called. It felt as if everyone's case but mine was being called. I ended up dozing off.

I woke up from the rambling sound that was coming from my stomach. Counting the days I'd been out of it in the hospital, I had not eaten in more than three days. My 140 pound frame was probably five pounds lighter now.

To get my mind off my hunger pangs, I filled my head with the words Catara had spoken to me.

"I feel it's in your best interest to plea out, considering you have a medical license to protect. You don't have a criminal record, but because you are doctor, the judge may try to use that against you. The whole 'you should know better and because you didn't do better I'm going to make an example out of you' mentality. It looks like your husband and"—she flipped through the file—*"Tasha Reese didn't file charges against you, which means the State has no witnesses. Again, because you have a medical license at stake, and the fact that I'm sure you want to get out of here as quickly as possible, I'd plea out of this and you can be home by dinner, because I'm sure I can get you released on your own recognizance."*

That sounded like a sweet deal to me. Before now I never understood for the life of me why anyone would ever plead guilty to something they didn't do. Now I understood just fine. I didn't care what they were charging me with, I planned on shouting from the roof top, "Damn it, I did it and I'm sorry. Now where do I sign?"

"Simpson, you're up," one of the guards said as he walked over to me and helped me to my feet.

When I say I almost passed out, please believe me. And it had nothing to do with being weak from not having eaten. My emotions were creating a storm inside my being that I could barely withstand. My only prayer was the casualty of it all wouldn't be my freedom.

Chapter 19

This shit wasn't like in the movies. I've been watching *Law and Order* for a hundred years, and whenever the judge ordered that the defendant was free to go, they were free to go. Their family and loved ones cheered, hugged them, and then took them home. That wasn't the case with me. I had to go back to jail and wait to be processed out.

As of now, I'd already been waiting four hours. I had a strange feeling that they were going to try to keep me locked up. I don't see how they could though; the deal had been made. As Catara had said, neither Dwayne nor Tasha were listed as State witnesses. Because I had a clean record and the State had a huge caseload, Catara pitched them a plea that they didn't even blink at before agreeing to.

I settled for one year probation on a vandalism misdemeanor, and I had to agree to six anger management sessions. No bail was set, as I was released on my own signature. Only, like I said before, I hadn't been released.

"So I hear you're leaving us," a male guard approached my cell and said.

"Yes I am, and I won't be back."

"Well, be sure you fill out the survey upon exit about how we did."

I twisted my lips as the guard unlocked my cell. "Sure thing," I said, knowing darn well I wasn't about to take my time and energy to complete a survey.

"Be sure you do it, as there is a chance to win a five-hundred dollar commissary shopping spree on your next visit." He began to laugh.

Fucker. I was so glad I was getting out of here.

As the thick body, African American guard stood laughing at his own joke, I glanced around the cell from top to bottom. I could not imagine in a million years ever calling this place home.

"Seriously, I'm sure you could use the money on your books for the next time you come back." The guard still had jokes.

"Didn't you hear me? I won't be back," I said.

"Yeah, yeah, yeah. That's what they all say." He whipped me around and cuffed me.

"Hey, do we really need the cuffs? I'm a free woman."

"Not until you step foot outside this jail can you consider yourself free," he said. He placed his dark skin arm next to mine. "Even then we ain't free, or are you eating too high off the hog to realize that?"

I glared at him in the eyes, mustering up a comeback that would cut his fat ass to pieces. But the last thing I needed was to get into it with a guard and lose my freedom before I even got it.

The guard escorted me down to yet another holding room. This release process was a bitch. They threw my ass in jail with the quickness, but acted like they didn't want me to leave. Damn! At least let me out on good behavior. I didn't bother anybody while I was inside. Hell, I didn't even eat up y'all's food. That's got to count for something.

My last step to getting released was claiming my personal belongings. It wasn't much considering I'd left everything in my car at Tasha's.

After that, I was actually able to inhale my first breath of fresh air as a free woman.

"Thank you, Jesus!" I shouted out, not caring who was around. I was thankful. This was a second chance for me. Things could have turned out far worse. I totally blacked out that night at Tasha's. Had I gotten my hands on her again, and had Dwayne not kept me from getting at Tasha, I could be here on a murder charge, or at least attempted murder.

I went to take my first step and then I stopped. I didn't have a ride, and even if I did have a ride, where the hell was I going to go? Going home could be disastrous. I don't know what I would say to Dwayne. Without having an anger management course yet, I was liable to pop off again, but not with Kendra there. Kendra would be that man's saving grace. I was not going to teach my daughter how to act like one of those hood rat, reality show chicks, even though that's exactly what I had acted like. Believe me when I say I'd learned my lesson. Something like that was never going to happen again.

"Can't call my husband," I said to myself. "Can't call my best friend because she's sleeping with my husband." I wouldn't even consider being in their presence at this point, let alone breathing the same air as them in a vehicle. I had to figure something out.

I thought about calling Tracy, but then realized I didn't even have my cell phone. I turned back toward the jail. It didn't take me long to realize that I'd rather walk home than to go back in there and ask to use the phone. Finding a payphone these days was like finding a needle in a haystack.

I looked down at my attire that I'd changed back into after retrieving my things. I was dressed for fine dining, or as the guard had so eloquently put it, to eat high off the hog. I was wearing an outfit that more than likely was equal in cost to most of the jail staff's weekly salaries. They couldn't have cared less how I got home. Probably thought I was going to have a limo out here waiting for me.

"They finally let you out of there, huh?"

I turned around to see Catara exiting the building.

When I say she might as well have had wings and a halo, that's exactly what I meant. She had been a Godsend in more ways than one.

"Yes," I said. "And silly me, I forgot to call a taxi while I was in there."

"Oh, well, you can use my phone." She dug her phone out of her purse as she walked toward me. Once she arrived to where I was standing she extended her phone.

I simply looked down at the phone.

"No one to call, huh?" she surmised. "Let me call you a taxi."

Catara started dialing, but then I stopped her by placing my hand on hers. "No, that won't be necessary. My purse . . . it's . . . you know what? A walk will do me good." I forced a smile on my face although in that second I couldn't think of one thing to be smiling about.

"Don't worry. I'll pay for it," Catara insisted. "I can't let you walk home." She gave me the onceover, her eyes landing at my feet. "Not with those bad ass shoes."

We both let out a chuckle.

I accepted her offer and allowed her to call me a taxi.

Catara placed the call and then tucked the phone back in her purse. "They said he's right around the corner and should be here in five," Catara relayed to me. She then handed me fifty dollars.

I looked down at the money and let out a sigh. "Here I'm the one who should be paying you for your services, and you're giving me money." I shook my head.

"It's okay. We sisters have to look out for one another.

Help keep each other sane, right?" She smiled.

I clutched the money in my hand, gracefully accepting it. "Right." I looked up at this giving woman who I hadn't even known twenty-four hours but who cared about me, my well-being, and my life more than I had. This woman cared more about me than, according to my actions, I cared about myself. That was going to change, and I was going to start showing it in action, starting with getting out of my marriage and getting on with being a mother to Kendra.

"Thank you so much, Catara. I appreciate this more than you'll ever know."

"Oh, I know," Catara said. "Trust me, I know." She winked at me and then walked away.

By that knowing look she'd just shot me and that knowing tone she'd spoken with, something told me she knew from personal experience. Well, it looked like she'd gotten past whatever drama she'd found herself in. And if that sistah could do it, then so could I.

The bright headlights beaming right at me pulled me from my thoughts. I stepped back as the taxi driver pulled to the curb. He got out of the car and greeted me.

"Good evening." The older, white gentleman appeared to be respectful.

He opened up the car door for me, and then once he was back inside the taxi, I gave him my home address. There was simply nowhere else to go. After that, there were no words exchanged between the two of us during the fifteen minute drive to my home.

I wouldn't have made for good conversation anyway. I was self-absorbed with emotion. I know I come across as this I-don't-give-a-damn type of chick, but I do give a damn. As a matter of fact, I give two damns. I was honestly concerned about my image and reputation.

Once I arrived home, I paid the fare and then headed up my walkway. My car was in the driveway. Dwayne must have been feeling really bad about his infidelity. He'd had my car towed home instead of to a tow yard. A tow yard is exactly where I would have sent his car.

I was a ball of nerves. What on earth was I going to say to my baby girl when I saw her? But I guess the more serious question was what I was going to do to Dwayne once I saw him.

Chapter 20

Awkward wasn't the word for how I felt returning to work to all the side-eyes, whispers, and glares. Returning home had been a piece of cake compared to this, especially since Dwayne hadn't been at the house.

I'd been relieved to find Tracy at the house with Kendra. When Dwayne learned of the outcome of my case and found out I'd be returning home, he made arrangements to go stay at a hotel. Not wanting to uproot Kendra from home, he asked Tracy if she would sit with Kendra until I arrived.

Walking into that house and seeing Kendra sitting on the couch next to Tracy safe and sound while watching television gave me life. At that moment, as badly as I hated jail, I realized that I'd do life as long as it meant my daughter was safe and sound, living a good life of her own.

"Dr. Simpson," the nurse stuck her head in my office and said, "your first patient has arrived."

"Great. Let her know I'll be with her in a moment," I said before the nurse disappeared on the other side of the door.

Wasn't that just about nothing? For once I'd been waiting on a patient instead of a patient waiting on me. I was dead serious when I said I was turning over a new leaf. Time in jail or a near death experience will do that to a person. I felt like I'd experienced both. Besides, I already knew folks at work were going to have something to talk about. I didn't need to add to the fact that I was an almost felon by having the nerve to be late on top of that.

I spent the morning taking care of my patients. I ended up taking lunch late because one of my patients went into premature labor, arriving at the hospital just as I was about to head out for lunch. We managed to get her checked-in and stopped her labor pains with Terbutaline, so two hours behind schedule, I was finally able to head down to the cafeteria.

Why hadn't I thought to pack my lunch? I felt like every eye in the cafeteria was on me along with every mouth. Okay, so maybe I was imagining most of it in my head, but I was certain I'd caught a couple of the nurses staring at me and had heard my name being whispered a time or two. It was so bad that I carried my tray of food back up to my office and ate with my door closed.

I did not want to be seen or have to deal with the whispers bouncing off the hospital walls, whether they were real or all in my head. All I wanted was to get through my workday and go home, at least for the next three weeks, because that was the agreement. I had put in my resignation via email this morning before the hospital had a chance to terminate me, per Catara's advice. I followed that up with a written resignation with my original signature, of which I delivered to Human Services prior to heading to my office.

I had also scheduled my first anger management class to be this evening. I needed to get those done and over with so that they did not interfere with me leaving for Cleveland.

Although I had not spoken to Dwayne, it was inevitable that I would eventually have to. I didn't even know if he was working today; him or Tasha. Ordinarily I would have seen them during lunch, but since I took mine later than usual, that didn't happen.

I thank God for Tracy and her sister. Even before this

huge fiasco, they helped care for Kendra. Some days Kendra came to the hospital childcare facility. That was no longer an option though. I didn't want to risk her coming here and hear something she didn't need to hear from one of the other children. Adults were rarely mindful of the young ears that were around them when they were in gossip mode. And kids innocently repeated everything they heard. Kendra was asking enough questions as it was, I didn't need her to add to the load. Every time that girl opened her mouth I broke out in a sweat, even if she was simply yawning.

"Can we call Daddy to say goodnight?" was the final question Kendra had asked me last night before going to bed. Kendra had been doing so well health wise and emotionally. It had been over four months since her last hospitalization, which was back while they were in Germany. We could not risk devastating her, causing her health to be at risk.

I was stomped by her question as her innocent eyes stared into mine while she waited on an answer.

"Daddy's working," I'd told her. For all I knew he could have been. That's how I justified telling my daughter what could have been a lie. I'd done enough lying to myself. The last thing I wanted to do was start lying to my child. But the next to the last thing I wanted to do was call up Dwayne, which was why I was going to make a trip to Walmart to get Kendra one of those minute phones. I didn't want Dwayne to have to go through me to get to his daughter each and every time. I certainly didn't want Kendra to have to go through my phone to get to him.

What I am thankful for is that at least Dwayne had the decency to talk to Kendra and share with her a little bit about what was going on, and that he was leaving the home. That made it somewhat easier for me.

Speaking of leaving, once I wrapped up for the day, I

made my way to the hospital garage. As soon as I unlocked the door with my key fob, a deep voice scared the crap out of me.

"Denise Simpson?" A man wearing a suit carrying a briefcase began to approach me.

You already know I went for my pepper spray. Before I could spray him a good one, he extended a manila envelope toward me. "You've been served."

I accepted the envelope with bewilderment as the gentleman walked away with a proud strut, symbolizing he'd successfully done his job. Little did that rat bastard know was that he almost ended up blind.

"A restraining order!" I said as I read the paper that I'd pulled out of the envelope. It was an order for me to remain 500 feet away from both Dwayne and Tasha. "Dwayne and Tasha," I spat, yanking open my car door. "Like they are the couple or something." I got into the driver's seat and slammed the door closed. "I'm the wife!" I yelled, banging on the steering wheel. "They aren't a fucking couple. I'm the wife. Dwayne and Tasha my ass." I gripped the steering wheel with so much anger, but as I sat there and thought about things, I had to ask myself why I was so mad. I'd planned on coming home from Cleveland and ending my marriage. Dwayne had saved me the trouble, just as I'd wished for at one point.

Oh yeah, I remember why I was so mad; because I went to fucking jail in the process! And out of all the women Dwayne could have cheated on me with, he picked my best friend. That is the ultimate low. Not only had Dwayne not been in love with me all these years, but he must have hated my guts to do something that low. It was a painful blow. He could have slept with Tracy's sister and I wouldn't have tripped like that, but Tasha. Yeah, that's exactly why I was so mad.

I inhaled. "Breathe, Denise." I exhaled. "Get it together."

I started my car and thanked God that I was headed to anger management, because no matter how many breaths I took in and out, a bitch was angry as hell.

It only took me about twenty minutes to arrive to my destination. I'd been told to arrive fifteen minutes early in order to complete new patient paperwork. Of course that barely made it in one ear before it went sliding out of the other. I got there when I got there. I wasn't late, but I wasn't early, if you know what I mean. That, for me, was progress toward new beginnings. The old me would have been late, period.

"Mrs. Simpson, Dr. Baldwin is running a little bit behind," the receptionist said in such a sweet tone that if it was possible for ears to get a cavity, I'd be getting silver fillings in both of mine. "But that gives you time to complete all of your paperwork." She extended a clipboard with papers on it as her face donned a huge smile that almost seemed permanent. "If you have any questions, please, please, please do not hesitate to ask me. Both Dr. Baldwin and I are here to help you in any way possible. Okay?" She hung onto that 'Y' sound for at least three seconds as she stared at me with batting eyes in wait of my response.

"Okayyy," I replied, accidentally mocking her tone. It was just so freakin' contagious. I took the clipboard from her.

"Take a seat anywhere in the waiting room you feel comfortable," she said in her same cheery, sing-song voice.

I nodded and smiled. I was going to refrain from speaking, because that white cheerleader voice that had come out of my mouth just seconds ago was scary.

On my way over to cop a squat I had an "Ah-Ha" moment. I was in an anger management counseling office. Hell yeah that receptionist was going to be nice. She knew she was dealing with folks with issues; anger issues. I'm sure the last thing she wanted was someone coming through that receptionist window and pulling her through it by the throat.

It took me about fifteen minutes to answer all those questions on the package of forms.

"Does mental illness run in your family?"

"Have you ever hurt or killed an animal?"

"Have you ever wanted to or envisioned hurting someone to the point of death?"

Was a chick here for anger management or was I auditioning for a show on the ID Channel? Some of these questions were outright crazy. If folks that came in here were answering in the affirmative to some of these questions, the hell with being Buffy the sweet ass receptionist. They would have to drape me in a bulletproof vest and have me communicating with the patients through a bulletproof window.

I waited a total of thirty minutes before being called back by the doctor. I wasn't sure if that was some kind of test on the doctor's part, because sitting out in the waiting area for a half hour could make an already angry individual that much more angry. For me, it gave me a taste of my own medicine. So this is what my patients felt like when I made them wait due to my tardiness? Hmmm. I would always be more mindful of that in the future, because it didn't feel good at all.

"Mrs. Simpson, Dr. Baldwin will see you now," the receptionist called out.

Lord, Jesus, here we go, I thought.

Just that quickly my emotion went from being angry from waiting, to being sympathetic toward those I'd made wait all of my life, to being outright embarrassed.

They could call it anger management all day every day, but the fact remained that I was about to go see a shrink. I know that I'm human and that we all have our problems, but I'm a doctor. I'm supposed to help fix other people, not get fixed. I couldn't imagine what my patients would think of me if they knew the person's hands they were entrusting their unborn children's lives to couldn't even handle her own life.

"It's right that way." The receptionist pointed to the door I was to walk through after realizing that I hadn't responded to her announcement.

I looked to her. "Thank you." I swallowed hard and then stood. I walked over to the door. I placed my hand on the knob and then entered, wondering if this anger treatment therapy stuff really worked. I guess I'd find out if I came back through the door the same way I'd entered.

Chapter 21

I had to admit that after three sessions with Dr. Baldwin, I did feel like a change had taken place in my mental state. Was I this entirely new, completely changed woman? Absolutely not. But talking to Dr. Baldwin had helped me get a grasp on my life. He allowed me to admit some things about my life and the choices I'd made that I always knew, but had never acknowledged, let alone dared to speak on to anybody.

"On your paperwork," Dr. Baldwin had said to me at my second session with him, "you listed that you had killed someone."

I nodded.

"Is that true?"

My eyes began to tear up as I thought back to the day that would force me to have to respond in the affirmative to Dr. Baldwin's question. "I killed a baby," I'd said to him. "My baby."

I relayed to Dr. Baldwin the details of the abortion I'd gotten when I was a junior in high school. Back then I had friends getting fake IDs to get into clubs. I was getting a fake ID to get an abortion.

By the time I finished telling Dr. Baldwin everything, I'd been through his entire box of tissues. I can't ever recall crying so much in my life.

For example, we got on the topic of my abortion, and

how that could be the deep seated reason I became an OB/ GYN. I wasn't solely trying to help the women bring a life into the world, which could explain my disdain for so many of my patients. I saw it as a way to maybe seek redemption for the life I ended. And in those young, struggling patients I saw what I should have been. Their fate should have been mine, and I hated being reminded of such. I hated who I was. I hated me. I'd spent so much time caring about whether I was in love with Dwayne and whether he was in love with me, when I should have been working on loving myself. I'd spent so much time hating my past that I never realized that was because I didn't love myself.

I found it so easy to talk about these intimate things with Dr. Baldwin. At first my guard was up because he was a man. How could a man possibly understand what I went through as a young girl and the after effect of it all as a woman? But he did understand.

Dr. Baldwin was a brother, which had initially thrown me off guard. All I could think about was Catara's saying in regard to behind every angry black woman. How could I sit and look into the eyes of a Black man when I wasn't seeing the Black man in that good of a light at the moment? A Black man had hurt me, so how could I expect this one to help me?

But Dr. Baldwin was easy to talk to and not once did I detect any form of judgment in his eyes, in his actions, or in his words.

From my experience, it was quite unusual for a Black male physician to be a Psychologist. They normally selected alternate fields of medicine such as Podiatry, Internal Medicine, Urology, Pediatrics, or Gynecology.

After attending four individual weekly sessions with Dr. Baldwin, he suggested that my last two be in a group therapy setting.

"Telling you my business was bad enough, now you want me to share my madness with strangers," I said reluctantly.

Dr. Baldwin assured me that I did not have to speak unless I felt led to. Although I did not know what to expect in the group setting, I wanted this demeaning chapter of my life to end. In my mind, I felt belittled having to be in a room with four other individuals who had nothing in common with me besides the fact that we were angry about something.

While Dr. Baldwin opened the session with instructions on how the group session would flow, I swept the room with my eyes, looking at the other patients as if they were beneath me. *They probably checked the 'yes' box to all those damn questions on the paperwork the receptionist had given them,* I said to myself. *I don't belong in here with them.* And I made sure to shoot Dr. Baldwin a look reflecting how pissed off I was that he had me up in here.

Just as Dr. Baldwin had told me, he reiterated to us all that we didn't have to share unless we felt led. "But if you are led, dig deep. Pull out and let go of all those things that have caused you to act out in such a way that has resulted in you being here today," Dr. Baldwin encouraged. "Pull it up from the roots and leave it here to die."

My body language demonstrated that of arrogance and pure rebellion. I crossed my arms and my legs, dangling my foot as if I was annoyed. I felt like a child in time-out for not obeying the teacher. However, once the stories from the other patients began to come forth, everything began to make sense.

Once I was engaged in the group therapy, I understood why Dr. Baldwin had wanted me to attend. Hearing about some of these other folks' lives didn't make mine seem so bad. That saying about misery loving company fared to be true. I didn't feel so bad about all my misery after hearing what some people were dealing with in life.

There was one man who had a deep seated hate for women. He'd been convicted of domestic violence charges. After his father died, his mother had treated him more like a boyfriend than a son. At the young age of twelve, his mother told him he had to be the man of the house, which meant he had to be her man too. And it didn't stop with him having to take on a paper route and find odd jobs to do for the neighbors for pay. It included him satisfying his mother's sexual desires as well.

It broke my heart listening to some of those other people's stories. By the second group therapy session, which was my sixth and final visit with Dr. Baldwin, I realized that I didn't have shit to be angry about compared to some other folks in this world. I might have walked into Dr. Baldwin's office my first visit angry, but by the last visit I was thankful and grateful for the life I'd been dealt.

I also walked away from Dr. Baldwin's office with self-control. After hearing one woman talk about how her kids' babysitter used to make them fight each other while she watched and laughed, I wanted to join her in whooping that woman's ass all over again. I was heated. I was calling the mother all kind of stupid bitches in my head when she talked about how she had now forgiven the babysitter. She stated how remorseful she was for going to the babysitter's house with a baseball bat and lighting her up with it, forcing the doctors to put the babysitter in a medically induced coma until the swelling on her brain went down.

She talked about how while she was in jail, her children were put into a foster home where one of them was mauled by the foster parent's neighbor's dog. She realized that had she handled the situation completely different from the start, in the end her children would all be alive today.

Hearing that gave me a change of heart. For now on, there

would be no popping off and snapping on folks. I would consider how it would ultimately affect Kendra in the long run. When the woman first started talking about how she went after the babysitter, like I said, I didn't blame her. I was all for it and would have went back to finish the job. But then hearing the domino effect of her actions and how she lost a child thinking she was protecting the child, I could definitely understand why she was remorseful. I now knew how to make alternate decisions when dealing with unexpected life events and situations. And as I felt my heart softening, I felt that perhaps I could forgive Tasha one day.

Even though initially in my mind that whole anger management stuff had been a joke and I was simply going through the motions, it had truly set me on a new path in life. With my move to Cleveland a little under two weeks away, it was perfect timing. New job, new city, new me, and new life. But would I simply be pouring new wine into old wine skin?

***

Moving day was only one week away. Cleveland, Ohio, here I come! No more Sentara, no more anger management, and last but not least, no more Dwayne. He may have hit me with a restraining order, but I hit him with divorce papers. Checkmate.

Catara had referred me to an excellent divorce attorney, who turned out to be her husband. No wonder ole girl could walk around in three hundred dollar play shoes. Home girl was paid!

Of course the day would come when I had to talk to Dwayne. We had a minor child together. Let's just say he'd better thank Dr. Baldwin that when he showed up at the house after only one week of anger management under my belt, that I didn't go upside his head.

He first called to ask if we could meet to talk about things the day after my first anger management session. He mainly wanted to discuss Kendra's and my move to Cleveland. Initially I saw red when his name appeared on my caller ID screen. As a matter of fact, the first time he called me that day I didn't even take his call. I had to whoosah, refer to the pamphlet of relaxation tips Dr. Baldwin had armed me with, then call him back.

"Is it all right with you if I come by the house to talk, plus to see Kendra?" Dwayne had asked. "I miss her."

And Kendra missed him something awful. She handled Dwayne being out of the house pretty okay that first night, but after that, she cried for her Daddy. A little girl needed her daddy, especially one used to spending most of her time with her father. I knew better than anyone that an absent father could mentally screw up a girl. I remember wanting— no, needing—my father. Perhaps with a Daddy in my life there would have never been an abortion. There would have never been a loveless marriage. There would have never been infidelities. A life of resentment. I wasn't holding onto all those what ifs anymore. I left them all back at Dr. Baldwin's office. I wasn't over it, but I wasn't angry about it. I'd learned the difference.

"I'm not sure you coming here would be such a good idea," I had said to Dwayne over the phone, "considering you and your girlfriend have a restraining order on me." I was being a bitch. I had every intention of letting him see Kendra, but the passive aggressiveness rearing its ugly head wouldn't allow me to make it easy. I was still working on that trait, which was a whole other pamphlet to conquer.

"How many times do I have to tell you that nothing happened between me and Tasha?"

I felt myself getting a little anxious, so I used one of the tools I'd learned in anger management. "Can we table this discussion until I feel I'm in a better place to discuss it? When that time comes, I'll let you know."

Dwayne obliged my request. He ended up coming by a couple days later, actually the same evening of my second anger management session.

Dr. Baldwin had armed me with a few techniques that had allowed me to have a calm, adult conversation with Dwayne. One of those things was to allow him to say everything he needed to say without interrupting. I gave Dwayne permission to discuss whatever he wanted about Kendra's and my move, but I wasn't ready to address his infidelity with Tasha. Dwayne obliged.

I was so proud of myself. I didn't allow my mind to wander any place other than the subject matter we agreed to discuss. If something Dwayne said struck a nerve, I bit my tongue. By the time it was my turn to speak, my anger had tapered somewhat. This really came in handy when Dwayne had the nerve to say, "You should be ashamed for the way you acted at Tasha's house. You owe me for talking her out of pressing charges on you."

While he continued to talk, I called him all kinds of sons of bitches in my head. I got it all out without having to vocalize it to him. Besides, Kendra was home. We'd sent her off to her room, but she was in the house no less. She'd never witnessed a single argument between Dwayne and me. So even though I'd shown some screwed up ways of communicating here lately, I refused to pass it on to my daughter so that she could pass it on to hers, and so on. I was nipping that kind of family curse in the bud before it could even think about blooming. Kendra truly was my saving grace in more ways than one.

When I was initially contacted by Rainbow for an interview, I felt the timing was all wrong, but who knew everything would end up being so right?

Dwayne wasn't going to contest the divorce. I wanted nothing from him and he wanted nothing from me. We had no joint assets together. We never even had joint bank accounts. It was safe to say that we were barely joined in marriage. He actually agreed to buy my home from me here in Virginia. That was another plus for Kendra, because it wasn't like she was giving up another home to move to the next. Whenever it was her turn to stay with Dwayne, which we agreed would be summer and all the other school breaks, at least she'd be familiar and comfortable with this home and not have to get used to yet another place.

For the past week Kendra had been in a sports summer camp that I had learned about. She'd really been enjoying it. It kept her mind off of Dwayne's and my split. It allowed me to get all of the packing done, especially since I was no longer working at the hospital. I can't thank God enough for working out a departure that didn't consist of me being fired.

The sudden ringing of my cell phone interrupted some packing I had been doing.

"Well speak of the devil," I said to myself when I saw the name of Sentara Hospital on my caller ID screen. I couldn't imagine what they might need. This was their second time calling me since I'd clocked out for my last and final time. I'd spent all of last week there showing my replacement the ropes. They were not about to start pestering me.

As the phone continued ringing, I decided not to answer it. I'd promised myself I was going to put a huge dent in my packing today. How was I supposed to do that if I kept getting interrupted? I'm sure they wanted me to do something. I did not want my day thrown off by what was probably my replacement calling me about one of those ghetto problem patients. No sooner than that thought crossed my mind did I picture Dr. Baldwin standing there wagging a finger at me.

"Oh, all right," I said as if I was actually talking to the good doctor himself. "Hello," I said, reluctantly deciding to answer the phone.

I stood frozen as I listened to the words of the caller. "Whoa, hold up? Are you sure? Why didn't anyone call me before now? Just forget it. I'm on my way."

That quickly my life was about to take another turn, and not just for the worse, but for what could be the worst ever.

Chapter 22

Where is she? Kendra Simpson? I'm her mother, Den-"
"Yes, Dr. Simpson. She's right this way," the intake nurse at the ER said.

I'd bypassed all those waiting in the line and ran straight up to the intake desk. Being an employee—or should I say ex-employee—of the hospital had its perks, and when it really counted no less.

"Well ain't that a bitch?" I heard someone in line fuss as the nurse got up from the desk to personally escort me to the examination room area.

Prior to my anger management sessions, had I been standing in that line and someone ditched in, I would have been popping off too. Right now I couldn't have cared less about any type of etiquette. I needed to see about my baby.

"How is she?" I asked the nurse as we hustled through the corridors.

"I'll be honest with you, Dr. Simpson. She was in extreme pain when she first arrived. Her counselor at the camp said right before lunch she'd started complaining and it got so bad where she wouldn't even respond to them. It was as if the pain had her in shock."

"Oh, Jesus. My baby." I was trying my best to keep it together. As a doctor, I'd witnessed a great deal of tragedies, including parents who gave birth to a live baby who never made it out of the hospital alive due to complications. I recall having to appear stoic and unemotional when breaking the news to them. One would have thought I was immune to situations like this, but let me tell you, it was something totally different when the child's life at stake was that of my own.

"We've gotten her pain under control, but she's scared. She's been asking for her mommy and daddy."

"Well, I'm here now. I'm here," I said as the nurse and I cut a corner so fast that we almost crashed into a poor aid pushing a supply cart. "Is her father here by any chance?"

"No," the nurse said.

My first instinct was to call Dwayne, but I didn't want to be on the phone with him while trying to see about my baby. And I wasn't about to make her wait until I got finished talking to him. She was going to get my undivided attention. I know my baby had been scared to death up here all alone waiting on somebody to come be by her side. Well, I was not about to make her wait any longer. Besides that, had we already been living in Cleveland, what good would it have done to call Dwayne? He was my soon-to-be ex-husband, which meant I was headed down the road of single parenting. I might as well hop in the driver's seat now and manage without him. I was going to be a single mom residing in an entirely different state than that of my child's father, therefore, I had to prepare myself to do for myself. Not only that, but Kendra was going to have to realize that her daddy would no longer be a phone call away. I would soon only have myself to depend on, and so would she.

"Here she is," the nurse said as we approached an examination room. She stepped aside and allowed me to enter through the curtain first.

There was about a two second delay as I lifted my hand to push the curtain aside. I had to prepare myself for what I might see. I had to be strong for Kendra. No matter what was on the other side of that curtain, I had to keep it together.

Kendra's eyes must have been planted steady on that curtain waiting for one of her parents to come through it, because the moment I opened it, her eyes were immediately locked with mine.

"Mommy!" she cried out as tears poured from her eyes. I could tell they were tears of fear, pain, but joy as well.

"Hey, Mommy's baby." I walked over to the bed. "What happened, love bug?"

"I hurt. I just started hurting." She began to whimper.

"Calm down, baby. Calm down." I began rubbing her hair with my hand.

Kendra was crying her little eyes out. All she kept saying was, "Mommy, I hurt."

I continued to stroke her hair with one hand and wipe her tears with the other, all the while placing gentle kisses on her forehead. This helped to calm her down.

"Dr. Simpson," a male voice said.

I looked up to see a doctor walk through the open curtain. The nurse who had escorted me into the room must have gone back to her desk, because she was no longer in the room. I hadn't noticed her leave because all of my attention had been on Kendra.

"Yes." I nodded.

"Hi, I'm doctor-"

"Shaul," I continued without even having to read his badge. "I remember you from the holiday party."

He stared at me for a moment. "Oh yes." He snapped his finger in remembrance.

I wasn't sure if he was picturing my face or my ass, considering he'd caught me and another one of our colleague's guest making out in a limo. He'd mistaken the limo we were in for his own. The party had been at a fancy mansion and each employee had been provided limo service so that they could drink without having to worry about driving. When he opened the back passenger door, all he saw was my ass tooted in the air.

"How is she? How is my baby?" I asked.

"She's doing much better now," Dr. Shaul replied. "As you can see, we started an IV for fluids, ordered a stat CBC and a urinalysis. Kendra's H and H is extremely abnormal." H and H stood for hemoglobin and hematocrit. "Her results were at a critical level." This required inpatient hospital attention.

I was so glad that I was in the medical field and could decipher what Dr. Shaul was saying, otherwise I would have lost my mind. Everything would have sounded so ominous. Don't get me wrong, what Kendra was going through was serious, and she could have died had she not gotten to the ER on time and received the necessary treatment, but my baby was going to be okay. It was going to take some time for her to build her strength and get back to her normal self, but it wasn't a touch and go situation.

Once Dr. Shaul filled me in, he finished up by letting me know that Kendra was definitely being admitted to the hospital for an indefinite amount of time based on how well she recuperated and at what rate.

After about a half hour, we received word that a room had been assigned to her and we were then transferred to a private room. By the time Kendra got settled in, she had calmed down tremendously. She was even watching a kid's television network and giggling at the young actors' antics.

"Denise, how is she?"

"Daddy!"

I didn't even have time to respond to Dwayne's inquiry. The minute Kendra saw her father standing in that doorway, she just about jumped out of that bed, IVs and all. She probably would have hadn't I held her arm to relax her.

Her eyes were popped open and were the size of fifty cent pieces as she waited for Dwayne to make it over to her bedside.

"How's Daddy's girl?" Dwayne asked as he bent over Kendra's bed and kissed her on the cheek while hugging her.

Kendra threw her arms around Dwayne and squeezed. I could tell it was tight by the imprint she was leaving on his shirt.

There was an endless array of affection in the tiny hospital room.

"How did you know she was here?" I asked Dwayne.

He struggled to release himself from Kendra's embrace.

"The camp called me," he said. "They told me she was being transported to Children's, but clearly that wasn't the case. I was at the wrong hospital going crazy looking for my little girl. I can't even tell you how my heart dropped when the nurse at Children's was punching the computer trying to locate her. I thought . . . I thought."

Clearly the mere thought of thinking Kendra's situation had been fatal brought Dwayne to tears.

"I'm okay, Daddy," Kendra said, rubbing Dwayne's hand. "Everything is going to be all right."

It was a sight to behold watching the child comfort the parent, when it was the parent who was there to comfort the child.

"How's our little patient?" a nurse entered the room and asked.

"I'm not scared anymore," Kendra answered, full of personality for an ill child.

Us all being there in the room together was like medicine for Kendra. I hope she didn't get addicted to it, because in a few days she and I . . . Oh, no. There was no way the doctors were going to give Kendra permission to drive to Cleveland with me in less than a week.

"Dwayne, can we step outside and talk for a minute?" I asked him while the nurse kept a high energy conversation up with Kendra while she took her vitals.

"Sure," he agreed.

"Kendra, Mommy and Daddy are going to be right back," I said. "We'll be right outside that door if you need us."

"Okay," she said, then continued talking with the nurse.

Dwayne and I stepped out into the hall after pulling the curtain closed behind us.

I stood against the wall with my arms folded looking downward. I don't think I'd stared in Dwayne's eyes since that night at Tasha's. I didn't look him in the eyes whenever he came over to visit Kendra. I didn't look him in the eyes at court during our brief hearing. Catara's husband had pulled strings to get us a speedy hearing based on the fact I'd be relocating soon. It helped that the divorce was uncontested. It also helped that Dwayne no longer had a restraining order against me. It looked as though the judge was going to grant our decree of divorce.

Even though I'd felt like I'd come a long way since that night at Tasha's, especially after seeing Dr. Baldwin and all, I didn't want to risk my sanity. I did not want to look at this man and allow any type of anger to rise.

"So, how are you?" Dwayne asked me with great concern in his voice.

"I'm making it. Ready for a new life in Cleveland," I said. "Speaking of which-"

"I know." He looked into Kendra's room. "It doesn't look like she's going to be able to make the trip with you."

"I know. I may have to call Rainbow and either see about

starting later, or not taking the job at all."

I couldn't even believe that was coming out of my mouth. But I'd never choose between Kendra and a job. I'd never choose between my social freedom and Kendra again. My reason for leaving her behind would never be to get away from Dwayne. On top of that, I wasn't the only one who had a life. Dwayne had his. Our divorce included a custody agreement. He'd been playing nice thus far, but I couldn't see him allowing me to renege on my parenting duties already.

"You won't do such a thing," Dwayne said adamantly. "Kendra will be fine here with me. Remember, I've taken care of her by myself. This isn't my first time at the rodeo."

I nodded. "I know." Without even thinking about it I looked Dwayne in the eyes. "And I want to thank you for that, Dwayne. You've been a great father, which has allowed me to do everything I've wanted to do. Take jobs wherever and just up and leave. I've been able to do it knowing that my child was being well cared for."

"And you're still able to do that," Dwayne said. "You are going to go to Cleveland and start working your new job. Start living your new life. You deserve it." Dwayne took a deep breath. He looked down as if gathering his thoughts, then looked back into my eyes. "I should have let you go a long time ago. And I know that you know you should have let me go too, which is what you were going to do that night at Byrd & Baldwin Brothers Steakhouse. I could sense something from the moment you got off that plane."

That explained why Dwayne had started acting funny during the drive home from the airport. His male intuition had kicked in.

"When I'd called you and told you I'd meet you at the restaurant, my plans were to do just that, but then I punked out. I couldn't do it. I'm a creature of habit. I was comfortable with you, that and the fact I didn't want to be twice divorced, which meant I'd failed as a husband again."

"Dwayne, you-" I wanted to stop him from beating up on himself, but he cut me off.

"Let me finish, please," he insisted. "By the time I left the hospital I'd made my mind up that I was not showing up at that restaurant. I drove around for about a half hour aimlessly. I didn't know what type of excuse I was going to make, but I was not showing up. So when one of the nurses on my team called and asked if by any chance I could help one of her friends out, I hopped on the excuse to go MIA." He took my hands into his. "Denise, baby, I promise you that I had no idea that it was Tasha who was in need of help. You know how it is at the hospital. We try to help each other out anyway we can."

He was definitely right about that. I thought back to when one of my nurses reached out to Tasha when she hadn't heard from me. Sure she could have sat back and allowed me to be a no-show at work, but that's not how we operated.

"I'll have to admit," Dwayne continued, "that I was at Tasha's place way longer than I needed to be, and that was on me. I was killing time. I'd deliberately left my pager and cell phone in my car because I knew you'd be blowing me up. For years I'd been too weak to stand up and let you go, and that night had been no different."

I covered my face with my hands. If what Dwayne was telling me was true, I had messed up big time. My stomach began flipping as guilt suffocated me.

The phone call.

It came to remembrance the phone call Tasha received from the hospital when she and I were talking while I was driving to the steakhouse. That must have been the nurse letting her know about the information she'd forgotten to log in. My blood about drained from my body.

Dwayne was being truthful and I knew it. Now that all the dots had been connected, I could see the picture clearly. All he and Tasha had tried to do that night at her condo was tell me the truth, but I had refused to listen.

"Tasha," I said, tears forming in my eyes while I shook my head. "She must hate me."

"She was hurt," Dwayne said. "I haven't talked to her since that night, because Lord knows I didn't want you to find out we'd been communicating and you think the wrong thing about us . . . again."

I put my hand up. "Dwayne, I can't hear this right now. This is too much, and right now I need to focus on my baby."

"I understand," he said. "Like I was saying, leave Kendra with me. You can fly back on the weekends to check on her. Then once she gets better and the okay by the doctors, she can fly back with you. This isn't foreign, Denise. We've done it before. And if there is one thing we know how to do, it's to sacrifice for our child."

I stood there silently as I took in Dwayne's words. I wiped the tears that had escaped my eyes. They say everything happens for a reason, but did I really have to go to jail and sent to the crazy hospital? Did I really have to think that my husband had cheated with my best friend in order for me to finally divorce him? Did all of this really have to happen in order for Dwayne to let me go?

And what about Tasha? Oh my God. She hadn't tried to reach out to me, nor had I tried to reach out to her. That restraining order I'm sure played a part. I wouldn't blame her if she never forgave me.

Here I'd been wondering if my heart would ever soften enough to forgive her, and yet I was the one who needed to be forgiven. I wasn't going to try to address that anytime soon. There was just too much going on in my life. Besides, there was still the matter of the restraining order. Although my intentions for reaching out to her might be good and well, there was a chance I could be thrown back in jail by breaking that restraining order. I loved Tasha to death and prayed to God she would forgive me one day. When that day might be, only time would tell.

"What do you say?" Dwayne asked me. "Does all this sound like a plan?"

I looked at Dwayne and more tears filled my eyes. I felt so much guilt. He was standing there burdened heavily thinking he was the bad guy in this marriage, a failure, but I'd disrespected this marriage a long time ago. I'd failed him as a wife too many times.

"I'm sorry."

Both Dwayne and I said the words simultaneously.

We both let out a chuckle.

"I accept your apology," Dwayne said.

"But you don't even know what I'm apologizing for."

"I do."

Oh Lord, I thought. What had Tasha told this man about me? I didn't even stop to think that she'd been privy to some of my behavior outside of my marriage as a result of our girlfriend chats. It never dawned on me that she may spill the beans to Dwayne and burst my bubble altogether. Dwayne said he hadn't spoken to Tasha since that night at the condo, but what all had Tasha said to him before he left?

"You're apologizing for the same thing I'm apologizing for," Dwayne said. "I'm sorry that I didn't step up and walk away from this marriage a long time ago. You didn't either. The signs have been there for quite some time. But we both refused to free one another."

Dwayne had hit the nail on the head. Even though I'd

physically been thrown in jail, I'd always been there mentally while locked up in a loveless marriage.

"And now we're both free," Dwayne said.

I nodded. "Yes we are," I said. "And I accept your apology."

"Thank you," Dwayne said.

"Neither one of us can go back and change what happened yesterday, but we can make tomorrow better."

He looked up at me. "Can we start with today?"

I bit my bottom lip and thought for a moment. Kendra was still young, which meant Dwayne and I were going to have to be partners for years to come in raising our daughter. Only this time we'd be partners without a marriage license.

"We can start right now." I extended an olive branch to Dwayne in the form of my hand.

He grabbed my hand and pulled me in for a hug.

"I still love you," he whispered in my ear.

Although I didn't return the sentiment to Dwayne, I closed my eyes tight and said to myself, *I love me too.* And that right there was the newest beginning I could have ever asked for.

Chapter 23

The rebirth of Dr. Denise Simpson was no joke. I felt as though I was planning for a new baby to arrive. There were so may T's to cross and I's to dot. I had to arrange for Mayflower to move my things from Virginia to Cleveland. Fortunately, the hospital had corporate housing. Although they weren't paying my rent, they had a corporate account with these particular luxury apartments that allowed for an easy move in. More than anything I appreciated the fact that I didn't have to do an apartment/house search.

The utilities were all turned on and included in the price of rent. The only thing I had to worry with was cable, phone, and internet, and let's face it, those have turned out to be the most important bills to mankind these days. I had patients back in Virginia who were on Section 8 with a three day eviction notice, but had cable and internet. For real? Although they weren't that much of a necessity to me, I didn't want to go without them if I didn't have to. Thank God cell phone carriers had towers all over the map. That was one less service I didn't have to worry with.

"Looks like you're getting all moved in pretty smoothly."

I turned to respond to one of the movers I'd assumed was making the statement. I damn near dropped the toaster I was lifting from a box to place on the kitchen counter. "Dr. Thomas?"

"Are we really going to start that again?"

I paused for a moment until I realized what he was talking about. "I'm sorry. I mean, Bernard."

That's more like it.

I watched as he crossed the threshold of the doorway and into the sitting room of my already furnished apartment; another headache I didn't have to contend with. There was an open wall in the kitchen that allowed me to see into the living room, of where Bernard now stood.

"How's your daughter?" he asked, making himself comfortable on my couch.

"She's doing better. They released her from the hospital yesterday." Kendra's last set of blood work had revealed a normal red blood count, thank God. "My husb . . . my soon-to-be ex-husband says getting out of that hospital has perked her up."

"I'm sorry to hear about your daughter's illness, and your divorce, of course."

"Hmmm, I'm not certain I believe the latter."

He chuckled.

I placed the toaster down on the counter and then walked out of the kitchen, joining Bernard in the living room.

"I would ask you how you knew where I lived, but with this being hospital housing and all, that pretty much answers my question. But at least allow me to ask what brings you here?" I stood with my arms crossed while putting my weight on one leg waiting for a response.

"Wow, you don't seem that happy to see me. I, on the other hand, almost went through withdrawal waiting for you to return. I have to admit, you have the best p-"

"You can put that down right there." I had to cut Bernard off because one of the movers was entering with a box in hand.

"Yes, Ma'am," he replied, then did as he was told.

I instructed his partner that was right behind him to do the same thing.

Once the men exited the apartment, Bernard and I continued our conversation.

"It's not that I'm upset you're here," I said. "It's just that–"

"I know. You're busy. This wasn't a good time."

"No, it wasn't," I said. And it wasn't just the fact that I was busy that I didn't want Bernard at my place. In spite of the fun and wild evening we shared the last time I was in Cleveland, that was the old me. The last thing I wanted to insert into my new life right now was a man. I'd just started getting to know and loving me. I wanted to spend the next few months, even the next year, getting to know the real Denise. I'd filled much of my life up with male companionship because I didn't want to be alone with myself. Well, all of that was changing. If by chance I ever did remarry, it was going to be real this time. And what I knew for sure that I wanted when it came to a husband was for him to not be somebody else's. So that totally excluded Mister Bernard.

Bernard stood, and I was relieved. Saved me the trouble of trying to figure out how to kick him to the curb in the most diplomatic way possible.

"Well, I'll let you get settled in. Besides, it's not like I won't see you Monday when you start working at the hospital." He walked toward the door, then stopped and turned to face me. "But if you get lonely over the weekend." He raised his eyebrows up and down.

I was very appreciative of Bernard, as I'm sure he was somewhat persuasive in getting the other doctors who had interviewed me to agree to my hire. But hell, I had already returned the favor when I gave him some pussy. If he thought he was going to have exclusive rights to my home and my pussy, he'd better think again.

In reality, I knew I had to work professionally with him, but for now I was living day by day. The future was the future. I would have to live with the consequences of my decisions. That was something my mother always reminded me growing up. That was something my anger management course had reiterated.

"Have a good day, Bernard. Thank you for stopping by to check on me." I walked past him and held the already open door, a sign for him to exit stage left. "I'll see you bright and early Monday morning." That was my way of letting him know that I'd be just fine Friday, Saturday and Sunday.

"Anytime." Bernard leaned over and placed a soft, gentle kiss on my cheek. He held the kiss there for a few seconds before he pulled away.

Apparently my woman parts didn't get the memo about this whole new beginning thing, because I felt a tingle between my thighs that was all too familiar.

I watched Bernard walk away and clear the doorway before I ran over and threw myself on the couch.

"Jesus, give me strength!" I called out, because Lord knows I was weak.

A part of me wanted to call Bernard back and get me a quickie in before I finished all the work I had ahead of me. I could still get mine in while getting to know myself, right? Then again, Bernard was a married man. The old me slept with married men, not the new me. With that reminder, I got up off the couch and finished unpacking, which is what I ended up doing all weekend long.

Come Sunday I was all finished, but I was also all worn out. I had made sure I had cable installed, but I'd been too tired to watch any television at all, not even old reruns of *Good Times* and *Sanford and Son*. So I decided to treat myself to a Lifetime movie and glass of wine before I turned in for the night. I was laying off the Cîroc indefinitely.

After about an hour into the movie, I couldn't take it anymore. Here I was on my journey to be this brand new, strong, independent woman, yet I was tuned into a movie that made women look like weak victims.

"Oh well," I said as I clicked off the television and tossed the remote onto the table. As I went to turn off the living room lamp and head to bed, there was a light knock at the door. "What the hell?" I mumbled to myself.

I was about to yell out, "Who is it?" but then thought better of it. Just in case I needed to play as if no one was home, that definitely would have been a dead giveaway. So I tiptoed over to the door and peeked through the peephole. After looking out of the peephole, I leaned back. What I'd seen had put a huge smile on my face. No, I hadn't seen a person, but based on what I had seen, I knew exactly who was standing on that other side of the door. My only dilemma now was whether to open the door.

My fretting wasn't long-lived when I determined that opening the door would only be an issue if I made it one. I was my own woman. I was in control of my destiny. Nothing else could come of me simply opening the door unless I made it into something.

I looked down at myself. I was wearing a pajama gown with a robe, only the robe was wide open. I tied the belt tightly around my waist, and then opened the door. At first I simply stood there smiling, shaking my head. "You and those damn roses," I said.

The roses that had been held high enough to cover the peephole were lowered. There stood Bernard looking at me like he could taste me. The bad part was that I wanted him to taste me; spoon feed him all night if he'd let me.

He handed me the bouquet of roses that were identical to the ones he'd given me at the restaurant, only this time they were pink. Like earlier, he made his way inside my place without an invite. Opening the door and accepting the roses was one thing, letting him inside my place was another. But he hadn't given me that option. He was inside now. I couldn't be so rude as to kick out a man who had just given me a dozen of the most beautiful roses ever, could I? Sure I could, but I wasn't. I didn't want to.

I closed the door and locked it. As soon as I turned around, Bernard dropped to his knees and buried his face in my private bed of roses. There were no panties to push aside this time. The only thing he pushed was his tongue inside of me.

"Ohhh, Uhhh," I moaned in ecstasy as his tongue worked my clit while his finger filled me up.

As I stood up against the door and allowed Bernard's tongue and finger to use my womanhood as his playground, I realized that opening that door had been like opening Pandora's box, and something told me that come tomorrow it was going to be pretty damn hard to close it. *Fuck tomorrow,* I thought as the next words out of my mouth to Bernard were, "Fuck me."

I guess it was safe to say that I'd been alone with the new me long enough. The old me had gotten quite jealous. I'd wait until tomorrow to start anew, because after all, tomorrow's just another day.

The End

About the Author

Author D. Simmons-Corbett was born and raised in Aliquippa, Pennsylvania. In such a small town and with little more than the excitement of Friday night high school football, she began writing as a form of entertainment. Even then she couldn't keep her words to herself, sharing her thoughts by penning poems for and about her friends. Once word got out that there was power in her pen, she began receiving requests to write. While she was in high school, one of those requests included writing for the church she attended. Even though life stared happening, happened, and is happening now, writing has remained a passion of hers, so much so that she decided to go beyond friends and family, and share her gift of the written word with the entire world.

Tomorrow's Another Day is D. Simmons-Corbett's debut novel. If it had to be summed up in ten words or less, it would be "Sex and the City with a few shades of grey."

It's a known fact that authors write what they know first, research what they don't know second, and then lastly, make up all the rest. With a failed marriage, being a single parent, to finally ending up with the love of her life, this author has plenty to write about. Not to mention a twenty year military career. She's had interactions with different people from all over the map as well as adhering to many different cultures. With fact being stranger than fiction, her experience in the field of nursing could have been a book in itself, and now it is. Only this time it really is fiction, but with characters so colorful, scenarios so realistic, and scenes so vivid, one would never know.

Life's experiences have created a burning story inside of D. Simmons-Corbett, as she sat back for so many years taking in life while living vicariously through those around her. It only made sense that she created characters that readers could live vicariously through as well.

D. Simmons-Corbett currently lives in a suburb of Ohio where she's setting fires with her pen as it hits paper to form her next work of literary art.

Please visit the author at www.anotherdaypublishing.com or email her at dcorbett227@gmail.com.